Butterfly Summer

Toni De Palma

This book is a gift to you,
my reader. Once you have
enjoyed it, please review it
on Amazon and Goodreads
and pass it on!

XO XO

Toni De Palma

Butterfly Summer

TONI DE PALMA

EVOKE PRESS

An Ellysian Press Imprint

Dedication

In memory of my A'zi – una brava persona
and
for Stella, who is always a chapter ahead.

TODAY

1.

My mother is the type that just won't quit. Take now, for instance. I'm desperately looking for the shot-list I need for a meeting in exactly ten minutes. But no. My mother wants to know who came up with the idea for plant-based diets.

"Really, Anna. Take away the ham hock, and you've got pea soup that tastes like dirt."

"I suppose," I say into my phone. I rummage under a pile of unread scripts, a pile I've been meaning to read for the past two months.

"Are you even listening to me?" my mother says. My mother prides herself on her zodiac sign. Leos are, by their nature, bold and confident. They're also demanding suckers, something my Libra nature can't deal with right now.

"I'm hanging on your every word, Mom," I reassure her, but even I can hear the bullshit tumbling out of my mouth.

Butterfly Summer

Chalk this up to having lived and worked the entirety of my adult life in Hollywood.

The people-pleasing part of my personality creeps in. "Tell me again why this is so interesting to you?" I ask.

As my mother talks about her most recent doctor's visit, which revealed a ten-point spike in her cholesterol, I topple over a mountain of headshots, hoping to unearth my list. No luck.

Of course, any normal person would have a backup copy on their computer. Not me. When it comes to composing shots, I insist on being old school, meticulously hand-drawing each frame, referencing camera angles and light placement. All ideas that will go to waste, since, most reality television is created in the editing suite. But each of those thumbnail sketches is a tiny work of art and a reminder to myself that, while I've spent the last three decades as a Hollywood hack, I did once go to film school. Drawing is my way of telling myself that I'm not a total Hollywood sell-out.

Cheryl pokes her head into my office. "They're waiting for you," she says. As an assistant, Cheryl's better than a top-of-the-line Rolex. She keeps me on my toes, and not just when it comes to being punctual.

"Okay," I say, but my mother thinks I'm speaking to her.

"So, cholesterol be damned? I should just add the ham hock?"

"What? Not you, Mom! I mean, do whatever your doctor is telling you to do."

Cheryl stands in the doorway. She's been my assistant since I started at Prixie Productions, so she knows all about the mother-daughter waltz I'm dancing. She shakes her head, and the elephant earrings I gave her last Christmas swing to the rhythm of her laughter.

I place my hand over my phone and quietly mouth to Cheryl. "You could help, you know."

"Why? I love watching you squirm." And because she loves raising the heat, Cheryl adds, "By the way, did I mention Avi is on his second cup?"

Great! Just great! As if the man isn't combative enough.

"Mom, I really gotta go."

When I think we've finally resolved the whole ham hock debacle, and I can finally get her off the phone, my mother says, "There is something else, but now I forget." At eighty-eight, it's not unusual for my mother to have her fair share of senior moments, but today's not the day for a game of Twenty Questions.

As my mother tries to remember, I glance down at my trash can. On the top of the pile is an old fast-food bag from yesterday's lunch. When I reach under the greasy bag, I finally find what I've been looking for – my drawings, speckled with chicken grease.

There's no time to replay all the emotions that had resulted in my list ending up at the bottom of my trash can. So, with Cheryl at my heels, and my mother still trying to remember what it is she needed to tell me, I exit my office and rush down the hall.

Apparently, the caffeine has already kicked in because, halfway there, I can hear Avi's voice booming from the conference room.

"Mom, I really, really have to hang up now," I say.

For no apparent reason, my mother's rusty bell of a memory finally dings. "Oh, but wait! I remember what I had to tell you. Someone's made an offer on your aunt's house in Ischia!"

From her active community in New Jersey, it's as if my mother has tasered me. My legs suddenly stop working, and

3

my vision blurs at the edges. Cheryl, who'd been two paces behind me, collides into me.

"What's going on?" Cheryl says.

Hearing Cheryl's voice, my mother says, "Is that Cheryl? Put her on the phone. I want to say hi."

Cheryl, who is like another daughter to my mom, grabs the phone out of my hand, giving me no say in the matter. "Hey, Rita! What's going on?"

As my mother and Cheryl catch up, I attempt to digest the news about my aunt's house.

Cheryl talks loudly. Two nosy production assistants lean out of their cubicles and I glare at them, causing them to skitter back into their cubicles.

A moment later, Cheryl says, "I totally agree, Rita. Yes, I'll let her know." Cheryl hangs up and hands me my phone.

"What was all that about?" I say.

"Nothing," Cheryl says. She points to the conference room. "You've got to get in there before we both get fired,"

In the meeting, I'm only half-listening as I continue to mull over my mother's news. My aunt's house has been on the market for a very long time, ever since she passed away. Why has a buyer materialized out of nowhere now?

"So, Anna, what's plan B?" Avi says.

"Plan B?" I ask. By the way Sam and Avi are looking at me, clearly, I've missed something important.

Cheryl kicks me under the table. "An earthquake in Istanbul. Such a tragedy," Cheryl says.

"Right. A real tragedy," I say, masking my cluelessness.

"A week out . . . there's no way we can film the finale there now. So, whaddaya got for us?" Sam says.

While Avi and Sam are the ones keeping our little *Bride-to-Be* franchise pumping out cash from year to year, Jacob and I are boots-on-the-ground types of producers, who have to make sure our production train doesn't fall off its tracks. But an earthquake one week away from shooting? This is disastrous!

I glance over at Jacob. Instead of tossing me a life preserver, he just sits there, looking at his cuticles, looking checked-out. There might be some truth to the rumor that Jacob's been interviewing with other production companies.

Avi leans forward, his annoyance, along with the well-developed traps he's perfected at the gym, pulling at the seams of his shirt. "Seriously, Anna? You've got nothing?"

The sweat under my armpits turns clammy. It's Cheryl who throws me an unexpected lifeline, but it's a lifeline I definitely would rather not have.

From her bag, she slips out a well-worn Manila envelope. The last time I saw this envelope it was tucked under some folded blankets, hidden away in the ottoman in my living room. How had Cheryl squirreled it out of my house?

Cheryl slides the envelope to the all-boys' side of the table.

As Avi and Sam and even Jacob pour over the magazine and news clippings I'd been collecting for years, my heart squeezes in my chest. Why is Cheryl throwing me under the bus like this?

"Beautiful little island," Avi says. "How do you pronounce it?"

"*Ee-ski-a.* It's in the bay, just off the coast of Naples," Cheryl says. Over the years I've gone to bat for her often, not only getting her raises and bonuses, but also talking her up to Avi and Sam. They know how valuable her contributions to the show are. It's a decision I am currently regretting because Avi and Sam nod appreciatively as Cheryl becomes Ischia's biggest cheerleader.

"Anna's father was born in Ischia. But did you also

know that Robert De Niro, Zuckerberg, Tom Hanks, and Rita Wilson have all vacationed there recently?"

My tongue finally comes to life. "We've already filmed three finales in Italy. One in Venice, one in Milan, and one in . . ." For the life of me, I can't remember the other place. Truth be told, if you've seen one *Bride-to-Be*, you've seen them all. "Why not shoot someplace more exotic? Ratings have been sinking, after all. This is our chance to wow our audience," I say, using the only language Sam and Avi understand. Money.

Cheryl, however is determined to undermine me. She turns her laptop around so everyone can see the screen, which now displays a comprehensive graph of every season we've filmed. It's a lot of seasons and Cheryl's made a point to underscore her point by highlighting the ratings from the finales that were shot in Italy.

"As you can see the three finales that were shot in Venice, Milan, and Bari, were our highest rated shows," Cheryl says.

Bari! How could I forget the overnight dates we filmed in that cute little Trulli house?

Sam turns to Jacob. "What about you, Jay? Have any thoughts?"

Jacob shrugs. The guy, who is usually pretty chill from all the yoga he does, is even more checked out than he usually is. Maybe he has already signed with another company, and he's just biding his time, waiting on the bonuses we get once we wrap. Though I doubt we'll be seeing any bonus this year based on our stats. Cheryl's right. We do need something extraordinary to entice our tired audience.

"What about Iceland?" I suggest. "The Northern Lights would be a fantastic backdrop. Just think how cute our couple will look canoodling in an igloo."

No one reacts, and I realize I'm just babbling now. But there's just no way I will ever step foot back in Ischia.

Avi laments about how pricey Italy is and about all the money we've laid out for the preproduction costs already for the Türkiye shoot.

It seems as though Avi is starting to lean toward my Iceland idea.

Cheryl, my uber annoying assistant, hammers the final nail in my coffin. "The finale doesn't have to be expensive. March is the off season in Italy. And did you know that Anna still has her family home there? It also happens to be vacant."

"Is that so?" Sam says, his interest in Italy suddenly renewed. "Is it one of those big villas with the beautiful flowers climbing up its walls?"

Like me, Sam is a frustrated creative. In his youth, before the Hollywood machine swallowed him too, he loved to paint.

"Nope. Not a villa," I say. While I'm sorry to disappoint Sam, I see it as a possible out. "It's just a simple family home. Believe me, it won't pop on screen."

"Still, we could use it to house crew or, at least hold equipment. That would shave money off the budget," Avi says. "I say we do it!" Since Avi gets the final word, just like that the deal is done.

The minute my office door shuts behind us, I let loose on Cheryl. "What the hell are you thinking?"

Cheryl kicks off her heels and flops down on the soft, shag throw rug she bought me last Christmas. Normally, I like when Cheryl makes herself comfortable, but today she's made herself a little too comfortable, in my opinion.

"Why are you freaking out?" she says, massaging the balls of her feet. "Your mother said that you need to be in Ischia next week to sign the papers, so I just figured—"

Butterfly Summer

"You just figured?" I say, not giving her the chance to finish her thought. But since Cheryl is the only person I've ever bared my soul to about what happened the summer I was seventeen, I feel entitled to stand up for myself.

Cheryl tucks her feet under her and looks up at me. "Listen, I know you feel like I threw you under the bus, but it's only because I care." From this angle I can see the flash of amber in Cheryl's brown eyes. And because I know those amber sparks reveal themselves only when Cheryl is feeling truly passionate about something, the temperature on my outrage is lowered a notch.

Still, Cheryl should not have made the decision for me.

"You know, Anna, if you don't go back, there's just no chance of ever moving forward." Cheryl holds my gaze a little longer than usual. It's as if she's waiting for the meaning behind her words to finally sink in.

And they do.

"Fine! You win," I say with an exasperated sigh. No one else in my life has ever been able to wear me down quite like Cheryl.

To her credit, Cheryl doesn't gloat. She simply nods, a bit more emphatically than usual. The up and down motion of her head causes her elephant earrings to swing, setting off a tiny stampede.

2.

As the hydrofoil taking me from the mainland of Naples to Ischia bounces against the white water of the Bay of Naples and sea spray shoots down the glass window next to my seat, I'm reminded why March is considered the low season. This is the time of year when the sea holds the frigidity of winter, and the frothy waves kiss the low, gray clouds that dip low on the horizon. If I didn't know any better, I'd say the sea is angry to see me back. Can I blame it after the awful mess I left things the last time I was here?

"Excuse me. Are you American?" a voice says from the seat behind me.

Turning, I peer through the space between the seatbacks. Two eyeballs peer back.

"I am," I say to the two eyeballs.

A moment later, a middle-aged woman comes around and settles down in the seat next to me.

"I could tell," the woman says, pointing at my e-reader. "Have you noticed that, when it comes to books, Italians are still kind of behind the times?" She doesn't even try to hide her disdain.

Personally, I also prefer old-fashioned pulp and ink. However, lugging thirty pounds of books across nine times zones is highly impractical. Maybe it's the Italian blood coursing through my veins. I want to defend my heritage's reading choices, but I stop myself. There will be bigger issues to address once I reach the island. For now, I like the distraction this woman's pettiness offers.

"Would you mind translating my order to the *barista* for me?" she says, pointing. Beyond the rows of seats, there is a long counter where passengers can order coffee and snacks. "I've tried a couple of times, but the guy's a complete moron."

Before I left L.A., Cheryl ordered me some compression socks.

"You don't want to throw a clot mid-air," she'd said.

The socks, while a nice sentiment on Cheryl's part, had only reminded me how young and without need of compression socks I was the last time I traveled here, forty years ago.

Kind gesture aside, I'd conveniently forgotten to wear the socks. Now my feet and legs are killing me.

"Sure. I could use a stretch," I tell the woman.

We sidle up to the counter where a few other people are waiting on their orders. Regardless of the fact that he has people waiting, the sole barista looks cool and relaxed.

"There really is no sense of urgency here, is there?" the woman says. Her long, brittle hair is spooled around her head like a skein of yarn, and she is wearing a quilted Patagonia vest and Timberline boots.

"First time in Italy?" I ask. Though the answer seems pretty obvious. But, if life has taught me anything, it's that you should never assume anything about a person. Not even yourself.

"*La dolce vita*, right?" she says, her tone deeply cynical. Earthy outfit aside, this woman, like so many others I've met in my life, is someone who tells herself that she has the bandwidth to accept that which is different, when, in reality, a disruption to their status quo, sends them into a complete tailspin.

The barista finally makes his way to us. I'm eager to detach myself from Ms. Patagonia and, without thought, I quickly and efficiently rattle off the woman's much too complicated coffee order.

The barista has chiseled features and a strong nose, and he resembles a boy I once knew a long time ago. He shoots me a confused look, to which I shrug; a gesture that silently says, what can I say? Do your best.

While it had been my intention to order her coffee and part ways, the woman refuses to let me go. "Your Italian is quite good. I've been listening to podcasts for months, and I can barely ask for directions to the bathroom. How did you get so good?"

The real answer to this question is far too intimate. Instead, I simply say, "I learned a little here and a little there." But a pang of guilt shoots through me. "Actually," I admit. "It was my A'zi who taught me."

"A'zi ? Is that Arab?" she says, with a deep frown.

The smell of this woman's xenophobia mixed with her Patchouli is enough to make my head spin. I'm about to explain to this woman that A'zi is Neapolitan for aunt when my phone pings.

"I've got to get this," I tell the woman.

Grateful for the interruption, I walk out onto the hydrofoil's exterior deck. A few other intrepid travelers stand in the dampness. I make my way along the steel decking, my shoes sliding a bit. Once I've reached the rail and can hold on without any danger of being pitched overboard, I read the text. It's from Avi.

> Avi: *How's it going by u? Any updates on the deets?*

I look at the time stamp on Avi's message. Calculating the nine-hour time difference, I see that it was four in the morning, L.A. time, when he wrote it. Knowing it's not unusual for Avi to get two hours of sleep a night, I text back.

> Anna: *Approaching the island and all good. I'll keep you in the loop.*

Avi responds with an immediate thumbs up.
There's another text, this one from Cheryl.

> Cheryl: *Grrrr!!! You didn't think I'd find the socks, did you? Anyway, make sure you take your vitamins! You know how grouchy you get when you catch a cold.*

Cheryl's text makes me laugh. Even from six-thousand miles away, she's still micromanaging me.
My phone pings again. Instead of Avi or Cheryl, this time the text is from my aunt's lawyer, Signore Pisani.

> Signore Pisani: *Very soon in my office. Yes?*

While his English is less than stellar, my mom has assured me that Signore Pisani is a very good lawyer.
I respond back to him.

> Anna: *Sí. Grazie.*

Signore Pisani: *The wishes for your aunt, may her soul rest in peace, be final and make her happy as I am also happy to meet you this afternoon at my office in the square near the fountain.*

Grammatical errors aside, as a lapsed Catholic, Signore Pisani's mention of my aunt's soul leaves me queasy. While my father never talked about it, it was an unspoken truth in my family that the reason my aunt's house has never sold is due to its sad legacy. Ischia is divided into small towns, where the problems of one family can be easily shared through a gossip chain. While I'm here to put my aunt's house in order, I'm afraid a few signatures won't erase the details of how my aunt died. It also won't erase the feelings of guilt I carry.

It strikes me as odd that, after all these years of sitting vacant, a buyer has suddenly come along now. Is it someone from the island? From what I know, there's been a downward turn in the market of late. So maybe the sad history of the house has somehow become easier to swallow now that the price has been lowered significantly. Whatever the reason, once the papers are signed and the finale is in the can, I don't want to spend any more time here than I have to.

But Cheryl's words – *If you don't go back, Anna, there's no chance of ever moving forward* – dig sharply under my skin.

For now, I try to remain focused on the practical details of this trip.

I text Signore Pisani back:

Anna: *The buyer has agreed to the delay, correct?*

I've explained to Signore Pisani how, due to my show's need for a location to film its finale, we will need to delay the closing by a week. As soon as we wrap on the show, the whole matter can finally be put to rest.

Signore Pisani texts me right back.

Signore Pisani: *Yes. No problem.*

My hand hovers over the keyboard of my phone. While it shouldn't matter, I still ask the question.

Anna: *I'm curious. Who's the buyer?*

There's a little pause on Signore Pisani's side. Maybe he's had to take a call.

Finally, three little dots dance on my screen. It takes a while, but in the end, just one word appears. *Anonima.* Anonymous. The buyer doesn't want anyone to know who he or she is?

What if the buyer is a Russian oligarch or a Sicilian mafia boss looking for a place to dump their ill-gotten fortunes? Or worse, a former child star, who wants to turn my family home into a toney Airbnb.

I tell myself that none of this should matter but, weirdly, it does.

It's the hydrofoil's captain that jolts me out of my thoughts. He blasts the horn, announcing our approach. There in the near distance is Ischia. Crowned by Mount Epomeo, a now dormant volcano, she looks as if she's been waiting for me patiently this whole time. While she may be ready to receive me, the feeling of ease is not mutual.

The motor goes from a growl to a purr as the captain cuts the speed. The momentum of the hydrofoil pulls us into the port's embrace. Coming up to our berth, two men on board fling heavy, water-logged ropes to a man waiting on the dock. As he tethers us to land, I start to panic as my past finally catches up.

JULY, 1984

3.

I've been traveling for eleven hours. My hair is flat, my antiperspirant stopped working five hours ago, and I'm dying of thirst. Where is that witch? Nennella promised me a soda forty-five minutes ago! Nennella is my aunt's colleague. The two of them teach at the same high school. But the minute Nennella met me at the airport, she soured on me.

"I'm being paid to deliver you, not your suitcase," she'd said. Was it my fault that my mother had stuffed my suitcase full of gifts for my aunt?

My father, unlike a lot of my friends' parents, is pretty old-school. The only way I got him to agree to me making this solo trip is if someone picked me up at the airport in Rome and delivered me, door-to-door, to my aunt's house. Itchy for my freedom, I agreed to my father's terms. But now that I'm withering in the sun, I might not even make it to Ischia.

Butterfly Summer

Having a few lira in my pocket, there's nothing stopping me from entering the ferry's cabin and buying my own soda, nothing except the hoard of tourists standing elbow to elbow on the ferry deck. Bumping through the crowd with my suitcase would be a huge hassle, especially in my current state of jet lag.

I stand on my tiptoes, peering over everyone's heads. Ugh! Where is that woman? During the entirety of the train ride from Rome to Naples, Nennella hadn't spoken a word. Instead, she'd kept her nose pressed to her *fotoromanza*. As she poured through her romance magazine, I stared out at the countryside flashing outside the train window. At seventeen, with no romantic history to speak of, I hoped that coming to Italy would clear some things up for me.

The door Nennella had disappeared behind swings open and, one by one, a very large, very merry group steps out into the sunshine. The group is comprised of two middle-aged men, three women, and a couple of rambunctious children, all dressed in shorts, cover-ups and those Dr. Scholl's wooden-soled flip flops that seem to be all the rage for people heading to the beach. I know they're heading to the beach not only because of the way they are dressed, but from the straw picnic baskets the women are holding. Long loaves of bread protrude out from the baskets, along with glass water bottles. Pressed to their chests, the children hold tight to their plastic beach toys, while, save for one man, who carries a net bag containing a precious set of wood-carved bocce balls, the rest of the men appear unencumbered, leaving the others to do the heavy lifting.

Rounding out the group are two teenagers – a pretty girl and a boy, who is far too attentive to be a close relative. The girl looks to be about my age. When the boy says something funny, the girl throws her head back. I see a hickey on her neck, and I know the two of us are worlds apart. The boy pulls the girl in closer, wrapping his arms around her waist and pushing his hands deep into the back pockets of her cut-off shorts. Watching their ease with each other causes all the inadequacies in me to float to the surface, reminding me again of the whole Jack Bennett debacle.

Like me, Jack Bennett was a junior this past school year. This year, we'd shared a lot of the same classes, but other than a group project we were assigned to in history, neither one of us had had much to say to each other. This suited me just fine until the day, my best friend, Alyce, told me she'd heard a rumor.

"Jack Bennett wants to ask you to prom, but he's too shy to do it," she told me. Alyce already had a date and she was desperate for me to go too. The days ticked by and prom bids were getting close to being sold out. "Ask him, Anna," Alyce insisted. But, unlike Alyce, who was really attracted to her date, I was pretty lackluster about Jack and the idea of having to put my arms around him in order to dance.

Alyce, however, is as unrelenting as my mother, so I succumbed to the pressure. The next day, I showed up at the tennis courts, where Jack was practicing his serve with the rest of the tennis team. He was wearing the same pair of dingy, white shorts he wore to gym class every day. Those shorts, along with the half-hearted way Jack glanced in my direction should have been the hints I needed to leave. But, instead of listening to the voice in my head, I justified Jack's indifference, figuring that Mr. Doren, the gym teacher, who also served as the tennis coach, would have yelled at Jack if he stopped serving.

So, I stood there like a dope, peering through the chain-link fence, waiting.

When Jack was done with practice, I waved him over.

Butterfly Summer

From his side of the fence, Jack said, "What's up?" His abrupt tone was not at all what you'd expect of a guy with a crush. But being new to these things, I pressed on.

"Uhm, would you like to go to the prom with me?" I said.

Jack looked down at the ground, as the rumor mill came crushing down on me.

"Thanks, but no thanks," he said curtly.

Jack walked away, the blood rushing to my ears.

On my walk home, the sting of humiliation quickly subsided, as I realized I was more relieved than hurt by Jack's rejection.

The next day, a new rumor got passed through school – this one true – of how Jack Bennett rejected me. In the end, Alyce went to the prom with her date and without me.

Alyce is sweet. She tried hard not to make me feel bad. "You didn't miss much," she'd said. But, at lunch one day, I'd heard Missy Prammer go on and on about the music and decorations and how she and Alyce and Alyce's date, along with Missy's date, Jack Bennett, had all had so much fun dancing and hanging out together.

I didn't blame Alyce or anyone else for that matter. The separation between them and me was something I'd felt for a long time.

It is why I am here now. Since backpacking through Europe on my own was not an option my parents would ever agree to, spending the summer in Ischia to practice being a different person, was the next best thing.

Not that I know who this different person is. Still, I'm hoping that leaving all that is familiar will give me some clues.

I continue eyeing the young couple. The girl shifts and her loose, linen shirt slides down at the collar, revealing her tanned shoulder. Her skin is smooth, without the tiniest imperfection or mark. She's beautiful.

Her boyfriend notices me staring, and I quickly pull my gaze away,

This time when the cabin door flings open, it's Nennella. She pushes through the crowd. In her hand she holds a small, paper cup that she thrusts at me.

I look down at the black, tarry liquid in the cup and frown. "I don't really drink coffee," I say.

"*Uffa!*" Nennella says, throwing her hands up in the air. "There was a line of people. You're lucky you got that." The sea breeze blows back the edge of Nennella's wrap skirt. An ugly blue vein snakes up the side of her thigh.

There's an expression here. *Non fare una brutta figura.* It's basically a warning that means a person should never do something that might bring shame to themselves or their family. It's a warning I've heard many times over the course of my life from my father. When he says it, it makes me wonder if he sees something in me, an aspect of my character, that might hurt his good name.

And since Nennella is one of those people who could easily give me a bad name, I drink the tepid, bitter liquid without further complaint.

The ferry captain blasts the horn and the rolling green hills of Ischia appear. As the whitewashed houses with their candy-colored shutters come into view, I forget all about my thirst. *This* is my reward for all my good-girl behavior.

4.

The mad rush we'd encountered in Naples is repeated here on the dock of Casamicciola, the town in Ischia where my family is from. Ischia is made of many smaller towns, all linked together by a winding, main road.

The dock is packed with the cars and trucks that come rolling off the ferry at the same time as the passengers disembark. At the end of the dock, a group of taxi drivers stand around listening to the soccer match on the radio, waiting for their next fare.

"Aren't we taking a taxi?" I ask Nennella.

"For a few blocks?" she balks. She keeps walking with me lumbering behind.

I follow Nennella through the main *piazza* where a large fountain gushes water. As we walk past, the breeze catches the spray. Tiny beads of water rain down on my arms, my head, my face. It's as if the island is blessing me.

Beyond the piazza, is the main *corso* lined with shops. The crowd is a mix of people. There are a few gangs of teenagers, who carry rucksacks on their shoulders, and rolled beach towels under their arms. At a café, we pass a group of men arguing about politics. Mostly, the corso is filled with women out buying the fresh meat, cheese and pasta they will use for the *pranzo*, the midday meal.

Unlike my mother, who does all of the shopping in one place, the women here float from store to store, each shop specializing in its own foodstuff. The *frutteria* has flat, wooden tables heaped with apricots the color of the sunset and straw baskets filled with heart-shaped strawberries. The sugar from the fruit is warmed by the sun, perfuming the air. The fish store has glassy-eyed fish caught that morning. The fish are draped over mounds of ice, their silver scales sparkling. And the *macellaria* displays whole, skinned animals hanging from hooks. There are also shops for leather goods, notebooks, postcards, and creamy mozzarella made from buffalo milk.

I was eight years old the last time I visited Ischia with my parents, so the corso is part of my childhood memories. But now that I am on my own, it feels more exotic and exciting.

We arrive at my aunt's house. Nennella taps on the buzzer and yells up to the second floor. "Maria!"

My aunt's house is three stories, with a wraparound balcony in between the first and the second floors. Cream-colored, with floor-to-ceiling, pine-green shutters, the house is bland compared to its neighbors'. From its position, right on the main road and with a straight view to the sea, as a child, my dad could sit on that balcony, having conversations with his friends, who passed by on the street below. The balcony was also my grandmother's perch where she was able to keep a keen eye on her children when the German soldiers appeared on the island during the war.

Butterfly Summer

Nennella hits the buzzer again. "Mareeeee!"

"The shutters are closed. Maybe she's out," I say, imagining my aunt milling around with the other women we've seen shopping. Why else would the house be locked up on such a warm day?

"You obviously don't know your aunt." While Nennella's tone is sharp, she also happens to be right. What I know of my aunt is limited. Other than the few, hazy vacation memories I have from when I was a kid, my aunt is a staticky voice coming through the Radio Shack speaker my dad hooks up to our phone every Easter and Christmas. Maybe my father should have splurged for the more expensive speaker. Because most times, the voice that wishes us Merry Christmas back sounds more like Darth Vader instead of a woman in her sixties, who never married, and who lives on her own.

Across a narrow lane, perpendicular to the sea, sits a two-pump gas station. As scooters and cars zip into the station, a man nimbly works his way back and forth, chatting with each and every one of his customers as he twists off gas caps and fills tanks. The man notices me and gives me a wave. I wave back.

"Put your hand down. Signore Chiachiaron is not your aunt's friend," Nennella warns me.

Signore Chiachiaron translates to Mr. Big Mouth. By the looks of it, the name fits, but this chatterbox of a man also seems quite popular. As people pull in, they treat him like an old friend, often patting him on the back. People laugh loudly at his jokes and some of them seem to stick around a little while longer, even once their tanks are full. Why would my aunt find fault with a person like him? Nennella's clearly got it wrong.

Above us, one of the pine green shutters creaks open, but just a crack. I catch a glimpse of gray curls, but the shutter is quickly drawn shut again. The buzzer buzzes and Nennella pushes the door open. Once we are on the inside, everything that is noisy and light and alive is blotted out, replaced by the dark, musty foyer.

My eyes are still adjusting to the dark, as we begin our way up the stairs.

Nennella grumbles. "It's hotter than a tomb in here."

She's right. Despite the marble stairs, the heat in the house is stifling.

At the top of the stairs, the dark gives way and we find my A'zi. Dressed in slippers and a housedress that is completely bleached from its original color, she looks a lot smaller than the way my memories have preserved her in my mind.

My aunt seems to be wrestling with her own sense of time, when she says, "But how can it be? You're so big!"

Nennella, whose already limited patience has expired, has no intention to wait one moment longer as my aunt and I adjust to the idea of each other. She sticks out her hand and says to my aunt, "I did what you expected."

We're all standing in the living room, which is a multi-purpose room with a round dining table in the middle, a couch on one wall, and a T.V. on the opposite wall. My aunt's small writing desk is also crammed into the crowded space. That is where she goes to get a small, leather purse from the top drawer.

My aunt proceeds to count out a large number of lira to Nennella. It seems like a long time till Nennella is satisfied. When she is, she shoves the bills into her bra and says a quick goodbye.

While I'd wanted to be rid of Nennella from the moment I met her, her absence only magnifies the already uncomfortable silence. What makes it worse is the clawing heat.

Butterfly Summer

My aunt is the first one to break the ice. "Go and relax on the bed. I'll make you something to eat."

My aunt has made up the bed in the front of the house for me. This is the room that faces the sea. I push open the shutters just a little and a welcome breeze floats in, off of the sea.

The moment my cheek hits the pillow, everything uncomfortable about this day disappears.

5.

Morning light presses through the slats of the shutters, but it's not the light that forces my eyes open, but the sound of bubbly laughter.

As I enter the room, I'm surprised to find that my aunt's living room is a hub of activity. A tall boy is poking another with his pencil, while a girl with tumbling, brown curls that skim her shoulders, sits with her back to me.

At the sight of my rumpled clothes and matted hair, the boy stops his taunting and stares at me, curiously.

"*Ciao*," I say, to the group.

The boy lowers his gaze to my chest. He leans over to the other boy and whispers something in his ear. The first boy bursts out laughing, while the other boy, who is smaller and whose thick bangs fall low over his eyes, looks down at his hands.

The blood rushes to my face, and I just stand there, my mother's futile promise that some girls develop later than others rings in my ears.

The girl doesn't turn around. Instead, she picks up the biggest, thickest book from the table and hurls it at the two boys, clocking the ringleader in the arm.

"Ooo!" the boy yells out in protest, just as my aunt is walking in. She's wearing another housedress, this one just as colorless and bland as the one she'd worn the day before. Though I assume these are her students, the ones who require summer tutoring, she seems to be in the middle of cooking. She's holding a metal contraption with a round barrel where a couple of boiled potatoes rest. A crank extends out from the barrel.

"Arturo! Giovanni! *Fermatevi!*" My aunt tells the two boys to pipe down. "Do you really want to stay back another year?"

My aunt, her hand slowly beginning to turn the crank of what is some kind of potato masher, turns to me. "You must be starving. I left you something in the kitchen for breakfast," she says with a gentle smile. Along with my jet lag, some of the awkwardness between the two of us seems to have lifted.

"*Grazie,*" I say, thanking her for her kindness.

My aunt walks around the table, continuing to turn the crank, all while peering over her students' shoulders, checking on their progress.

I head for the kitchen, but not before taking a quick peek at the girl, who'd stood up for me. Her head is buried in her book, but she can't fool me. It was her laughter that had woken me up from my stupor. And now that she's revealed how tough she is, I want to know more.

In the kitchen, I find a dish. My aunt's idea of breakfast isn't cereal in milk. Instead, she's left me a fresh roll filled with prosciutto and fresh buffalo mozzarella. The mozzarella is still warm and, when I take a bite, the buffalo

28

milk runs down my chin.

As the food fills my rumbling stomach, I take in the details of the kitchen. It's tiny compared to our kitchen back home. A table for two is pushed up close to a single window, so anyone sitting there has a view of the street below. Like all the other windows in my aunt's house, this one is also shuttered.

I push the window open a bit and the noisy world outside comes flooding in. There on the street level is Signore Chiachiaron again, moving from pump to pump, laughing and smiling, just as he did the day before. He leans over, but gets tripped up in the fuel hose, and he almost loses his balance. For him, this is just another reason to laugh, this time at himself.

The sandwich makes me thirsty and I look for something to drink in the refrigerator. As I pull out a bottle of milk, I notice a small paper carton sitting on the side shelf. I flip the lid open and discover a dozen, glass vials, holding some kind of lemon-colored liquid. The vials are the size of my pinky, each one pinched at the end, sealing the liquid in. I shut the lid.

When I look up, there she is, the girl from the living room. She stands, with her back pressed against the wall, her hands crossed over her chest, watching me curiously as I pour the milk into a glass.

"How old are you?" she says. While it's a normal enough question, the expression on her face, along with the way she hadn't thought twice to throw a book at someone, makes me think there might be more to her question.

"Seventeen. Why? How old are you?" I say.

"Fifteen," she says, sticking out her chin. It's a gesture that speaks volumes.

While she is a full head shorter than me, this girl is far more developed. Her shirt doesn't gape like mine does but instead hugs her soft curves. Unlike my blemished face, she has smooth olive skin, and her chestnut-colored hair, sweeps across her shoulders with just the right amount of wave.

But what strikes me most about her goes beyond her physical appearance. It is how she carries herself, with so much pride and a complete lack of shame, that triggers the question I've had about myself ever since the year I entered middle school. It's a question that might lead to an answer that is wrought with so much *brutta figura* that I must push it away and desperately look for another way to be superior to her.

My chance to show her I am just as good as her comes when my aunt yells, "Delia! Come back here and finish your work."

Delia. Even her name sounds mythical. But, like all mythical creatures, Delia has her vulnerability.

I use her weakness against her, the way she's used mine against me. "You better go back, unless you want to be left back a grade," I say.

A sparkle of light is lit in Delia's eyes. Does it indicate anger? Respect? Whatever the emotion, a sense of pride warms my chest that I've been able to do this to her.

Delia, however, is not about to give me the last word. She shrugs, her eyes landing on the glass of milk in my hand. "You know, in Italy, only babies drink milk," she says.

A dozen responses come to mind, but she doesn't given me the chance. Without another word, she leaves.

Exasperated, I pour the rest of my milk down the drain.

6.

My aunt pulls another chair up to the round table and orders me to sit. She begins to search through her desk, pulling out a notebook, a pen, and a few index cards. Confused, I watch her as she goes to her bookshelf, where she considers for a moment, before selecting a slim book.

She sets the pen, notebook, and cards in front of me. With a heavy fist, she flattens the book open, the dried glue on the book's spine making a cracking sound.

"What's this for?" I ask.

"I want you to translate this story into English," she explains.

"But I'm on vacation," I say. "I want to go to the beach and have fun, not do schoolwork."

"If you think I'm going to let you go around out there on your own, you're crazy," she says. My aunt points toward the closed shutters, as if it's not just the sun my aunt is trying to keep out.

Across from me, Delia doesn't look up from her book, but the little curl at the corner of her lips as she smirks is obvious to me. This only makes me madder.

I glance at Giovanni and Arturo. Giovanni smiles wide, pleased as punch that I have joined their pathetic, little club. But Arturo's face holds a bit more compassion for me.

The book my aunt has selected for me is called *Marcovaldo* or *The Seasons in the City*. I've never seen a book with two titles before.

I thumb through a few pages. "This is too hard," I complain.

My aunt goes back to her shelf. This time she returns with an Italian-English dictionary. "Little by little," she says, not taking no for an answer.

Next to me, Giovanni snickers. "See, Arturo, you're not the only one who gets stuck with extra work," he says.

The tips of Arturo's ear turn red, but the boy doesn't say a word.

With no other options, I listlessly give it a try. It's dizzying, bouncing back and forth, hunting down each word. But when I have a whole sentence written, it makes no sense. Italo Calvino, the man who wrote the story, doesn't write like any authors I've read.

My aunt stands behind Delia, examining the page she's completed. "Brava, Delia. Brava," my aunt says.

Maybe I've become too obsessed with this girl, but I could swear that Delia is intentionally showing off just to rub my face in it.

It's another half hour of me not making heads or tails of the story when my aunt looks at her watch. "It's one o'clock. Time for lunch."

With that, everyone is released from prison for the day. Everyone except me.

Nennella was right. My aunt's house is a tomb. Once Delia and the two boys leave, the house is awash in a stifling quiet again.

"Maybe, after lunch, we can take a walk in the piazza?" I say to my aunt, as I set the table for lunch.

My aunt shakes her head and, after lunch, we watch a black and white movie. My aunt hardly makes it past the first ten minutes before she's asleep in her chair.

The next few days are a repeat of the one before it and the one before that. While I rather not be doing schoolwork on my summer vacation, at least having Delia and the two boys around gives me the chance to be with people close to my age. I'm even better at tolerating the smell of sweaty boys.

In those three hours up until lunch, I also get to spend time with Delia. If you can call sitting next to each other, neither one of us saying a word, spending time together. But, if I'm being entirely honest with myself, these last few days I've become less concerned with exploring the island, and I've spent more time thinking of Delia.

Where does she go when she leaves here? Does she have friends? A boyfriend? For me, Delia has become just as much of a puzzle as the story my aunt has given me to translate.

On the fourth day of my vacation, the pieces of at least one of the puzzles start to come together. As Giovanni draws lewd pictures on Arturo's notebook, making the poor kid squirm, I begin to see a pattern in Calvino's writing. Like a snake eating its own tail, I notice how the subject of the sentence I've been staring at this entire time is positioned at the end of the sentence, not the beginning. Calvino has built a lot of his sentences in this way. Now that I see it, the story gets easier to translate.

Satisfied, I laugh quietly to myself. Delia is the only one who notices. She briefly glances at me, which feels like a small win. Since we spoke in the kitchen, she hasn't said another word to me. The fact that she is ignoring me bothers me even more than the boring afternoons spent with my aunt in front of her T.V.

Unfortunately, Delia's interest in me is fleeting.

Before lunch, I'm able to suss out a few more details of the story. Marcovaldo, it turns out, is a man who hates his life in the city. As a factory worker in a dull, gray, industrial city in the north of Italy, he's bored. Apparently, the guy is pretty desperate for excitement because, when he finds some mushrooms growing through a crack in the sidewalk, he gets pretty excited. The mushrooms are pretty small, so he leaves them there in the open sidewalk, rushing home to announce to his wife and children that soon they will have a feast.

My aunt calls time for lunch, and I watch as Delia and the two boys begin to pack it in for the day.

"Meet me after lunch at the field," Giovanni tells Arturo. "Some boys are having a game."

Although Arturo doesn't strike me as much of an athlete, he promises to be there.

Giovanni looks at me and, for a moment, I think he might invite me too. Instead, he says, "Ciao." He leaves, followed by Arturo.

Delia leaves next, not bothering to linger a moment longer. And who can blame her? I'm not someone interesting enough to stick around for.

Even before I hear the sound of the door downstairs, shutting in place, my aunt says, "Set the table." And our usual afternoon routine continues on.

The next day is Sunday, which means no one comes to the house.

"Can we please do something today?" I say, realizing how pathetic I must sound. What other seventeen-year-old has to beg for a little bit of freedom with this much fervor? What other seventeen-year-old sits at home doing what is expected of her? Someone like me, who is afraid her father will cut her trip short if I don't do what my aunt tells me to do.

"You know, the mafia isn't going to kidnap me if I just go for a walk by myself," I say, attempting a bit of humor.

My aunt doesn't laugh at my joke, but she surprises me when she says, "I do want to take you somewhere."

Much to my disappointment, we don't end up at the beach or even go for a stroll in the piazza. Instead, a half-hour later, we are standing in front of a large, ornate, wrought iron gate.

"The cemetery?" I say.

My aunt ignores my disappointment. She walks onto the grounds, and I follow.

While it's not exactly where I want to be, at least I'm not inside the house broiling. The cemetery is actually quite beautiful with flowering trees and marble sculptures of angels, Jesus and the Mother Mary. The salt air blowing in from the water mingles with the smell of burning wax from the numerous candles people leave burning for their dearly departed.

Near the entrance, there's a tiny shed, a little bit larger than the booth where Signore Chiachiaron goes to make change or grab a container of motor oil for one of his customers.

Butterfly Summer

My aunt points to the shed. "Anna, get a broom and a dustpan."

As she takes a bucket from a stack of buckets leaning against the shed and starts filling it with water, I enter the shed, where I discover a bin of soil, old terracotta pots, rakes, and a few objects that seem out of place. One of these things is a child's plastic truck with a missing wheel. Without further thought, I grab a broom and a dustpan.

At my grandparent's grave, I have a faint memory of being here once before as a very small child. As my aunt cleans the grime away from the marble, the sweat pours down her face.

"Who's going to do this when I'm gone?" my aunt says, with such an intensity it feels like a slap in the face.

"I'll do it," I say.

"You?" my aunt scoffs at how ludicrous an idea it is that me, who lives three-thousand miles away, can uphold such a promise.

"Here. Fill this," my aunt says, handing me the bucket.

I do what she asks because I still hold onto the desire to be the good-girl, the one who never seems to know how to please anyone, least of all herself.

As the water increases in the bucket, so does my own frustration. My vacation is not how I'd envisioned it in my mind. Maybe it's time to call my parents, pretending I am homesick.

But, as I turn the spigot off, a familiar voice calls my name. "Anna!"

Entering through the wrought iron gate is Delia. Alongside her is a pretty, middle-aged woman, with the same smooth, olive complexion as Delia.

"Mamma, this is Anna, *Professoressa* Monti's niece," Delia says.

The woman smiles at me warmly, but before she can say anything, Delia says, "Go say hello to the Professoressa, Mama, and I'll get a bucket of water for you." Then, as if we've been lifelong friends, Delia loops her arm through mine. The feeling of her skin against mine makes me catch my breath.

The minute her mother is gone, Delia drops her hand and she begins filling a bucket with water.

Unnerved by how Delia's hand felt on my arm, I laugh. "So, this is what you do on Sundays too?"

"Oh, no. We never come here," she says, flashing me a secret smile.

The warmth in my body returns, spreading to the rest of me. This isn't a new feeling. Whenever Melissa George turned cartwheels in gym class, the sight of her long legs also sent shivers up my spine. But Melissa George was someone I merely observed from a distance.

The confusion that's been chasing me seems to have caught up, along with a seesawing sense of shame that my feelings should be applied to boys, not girls.

Delia picks up her bucket. She walks ahead of me. And, if I believed in such things, I would swear there's an aura of pure, white light surrounding her. It's the magnetism from this light that pulls me along in its current.

As we approach, my aunt and Delia's mother are deep in conversation. Delia's mother's pretty face is now marred by a scrunched-up brow and a deep frown.

Delia's mother turns on her. "La Professoressa has just given me an earful. Just wait till I tell your father!"

"Ufff!" Delia says, rolling her eyes and throwing her hands up like it's no big deal.

"Your father has to work overtime so we can afford tutoring. And what does he get for it?" Delia's mother pinches her on the same arm she'd curled around mine.

Delia jumps back. "Who can study in this heat!" she says, rubbing the spot where a small red mark is starting to bloom. "Look at Anna."

And, with that, everyone's eyes suddenly veer to me.

"What about me?" I say.

"The heat. It's terrible, right?" Delia arches her brow at me, then glances at the two adults. Her gesture seems to imply that it is us versus the two adults. The fact that Delia thinks there is an *us*, at all, thrills me.

"Oh, right," I say, fanning myself with my hand for effect.

"Yes, you should have stayed in America with your air-conditioner," Delia says. With the authority of an expert on such matters, Delia adds. "Everyone in America has an air-conditioner."

Even though this is not true and we only have one oscillating fan that just pushes the hot air around, I don't correct Delia because she seems to have some kind of plan. It's a plan that I hope will ultimately include me in some way.

While Delia's mother has no sympathy for her daughter, she finds some in reserve for me. "Maria, the child *has* traveled all this way."

Delia seems to sense an inroad and jumps in. "I can take Anna to the beach with me. You would like that, wouldn't you, Mamma?"

Delia's mother smiles at me gently. "I can see you are a good girl, Anna," her mother says to me.

It is odd to me that, after being in my presence for only twenty minutes, Delia's mother can conclude this about me.

However, no matter how good or not I am, I can't help but wonder why does a girl as confident as Delia need me as her bargaining chip?

As if to up the ante on her bet, Delia says, "And I

38

promise to only get perfect marks on my schoolwork from now on."

My aunt snickers. This isn't very nice. She should be encouraging Delia to do better. However, regardless of the spirit in which the decision is made, my aunt agrees, her consent coming in the form of a half-hearted sniff.

Delia doesn't do or say anything to mark her victory. And because I am quickly becoming accustomed to being content following Delia's lead, I bite my lip, keeping my elation to myself.

7.

Delia arrives promptly the next morning, ahead of Giovanni and Arturo. She quickly settles into her chair, going about her lesson with singular focus. Given her deal with my aunt, I am elated. However, she doesn't so much as glance at me. My return to invisibility status calls into question again what Delia really thinks of me.

For the next hour, Delia keeps her head down. Even when my aunt goes to check something she's cooking on the stove, and Giovanni throws an eraser at Delia's head, she doesn't flip out. She merely glares at Giovanni and gets back to work.

Following Delia's example, I set about translating the next paragraph of *Marcovaldo*. In the story, Marcovaldo's anxiety is high when he fears that someone else has discovered his precious trove of mushrooms.

Before I start on the next paragraph of the story, Delia shuts her book. "Professoressa, I'm finished with my assignment," Delia says, handing my aunt her paper.

My own anxiety shoots through the roof as my aunt checks over Delia's assignment. It has to be perfect. Otherwise, no deal.

Giovanni makes a face at Arturo as if to say *who does Delia think she is showing us up like this?* Arturo smiles at Giovanni, but his smile is weak and unconvincing.

Last week, there'd been a day when Giovanni had come an hour late to lessons. Without Giovanni around, Arturo was a lot livelier. He'd told Delia and I about the time his father had taken him fishing on his little rowboat, mimicking how'd he'd almost capsized the boat, by standing and flailing his arms. The three of us had laughed and Arturo's round, boyish face and big, round eyes revealed a sweet soul.

But around Giovanni, Arturo seems to shrink. He dutifully goes along with everything Giovanni says. It makes me sad for Arturo. But it also makes me wonder what people see in me when they look real close.

My aunt taps her red pencil. I wait for the pencil to take a venomous bite from the page, but the bite never comes.

"It's good," my aunt says.

"So, Professoressa? The beach?" Delia says.

Still a bit reluctant, my aunt nods.

For the first time that morning, Delia's eyes lock on mine. "Ready?"

Is it true? Am I really being set free?

Giovanni arches his back and groans, while Arturo shoots me a shy smile. At least, he is happy for me.

Before my aunt changes her mind, I race to change into my bathing suit. Then I grab the beach bag I packed the night before. Like two caged animals set free, we run down the steps, neither one of us wanting to waste a single second.

Butterfly Summer

Delia's bought us a few precious hours of beach time before the two of us have to get back to our houses for lunch. She walks briskly ahead of me, her rubber sandals making a *thwack thwack thwack* sound as they slap the cobblestone street.

As we make our way along the main corso, a lot of people say hello to her, telling her to give their regards to her mother and father.

I catch up to Delia and try my hand at an actual conversation with her. "It must be nice to live in a place where people know you."

My attempt fails. "You think?" she says, her tone clearly implying that I clearly don't know what I'm talking about when it comes to such things.

Delia, I am quickly realizing, is like one of those Russian nesting dolls that has so many, other layers hidden inside of it.

Delia quickens her pace, and now I don't even try to keep up. The fantasy I've created in my mind, I realize is just that – a fantasy. My suspicions were right. Delia seems to have no interest in actually *being* with me. I think about going back. If I return to my aunt's house, my aunt will surely tell Delia's mother and that will fix her!

But then we'll both be punished, and both of us will be stuck in the house for the rest of the summer. What's the point of that?

Swallowing my pride, I decide that if Delia sees me as her *get-out-of-jail-free* card, I can do the same.

Too wrapped up in my head to notice, we arrive at the port.

I'm confused. "I thought we were going to the beach?" I say.

"The beach is for tourists," Delia explains.

While it's nice not to be considered just a tourist, Delia's response does nothing to clear up my confusion.

The port is in complete chaos again. A large, passenger ferry has just docked, bringing with it another wave of travelers, cars and trucks.

A micro-taxi, bulging with tourists and their luggage, barrels toward us, Delia grabs my arm, yanking me out of the way. "This way," she says, leading me toward a high, cement wall that runs out to the sea. The wall is a good three feet above my head, making it impossible to see what is on the other side.

As Delia climbs to the top of the wall, I am still thinking about the sensation of her hand on my arm as she pulled me out of the way of the taxi.

From the top of the wall, her hands on her hips, Delia looks down at me. "What are you waiting for?"

"You want me to climb up there? Why?" I say.

"You wanted to go swimming, right?" Delia says, pointing out to the sea.

Swimming is one thing, but at the cost of risking my life? And with all these people around. What if someone recognized Delia, or worse, me and my aunt got wind of what we were doing?

As I deliberate my options, Delia loses her patience with me. She throws up her hands. "Do what you want," she says.

Delia walks down the length of the wall, getting about halfway. She jumps down to the other side, disappearing from sight completely.

A car passes precariously close, spewing exhaust from its broken tailpipe. My goal for this summer had been to push myself, to go beyond the limits imposed on me not only by other people, but by me too. Wasn't this situation exactly what I'd hoped for?

Though I still have no idea what is on the other side of the wall, I decide to go for it.

After a few attempts that result in me stubbing my toe and scraping my knee, I finally make it to the top. From up here, the wall isn't very wide, about the width of my arm, a challenge even for Melissa George's gymnastic skills. A jetty of flat-topped boulders that are jumbled in a big pile, butts up the entirety of the wall, creating a perilous path down to the sea. In the distance, I spot a few people sunbathing on the rocks.

The cover-up, which is my mother's, is two sizes larger than what I usually wear. When the sea breeze catches the material, it twists around my ankles, making the walk perilous.

As I come up to the point where Delia disappeared, I hear the voice of a boy yell up to me. "Ciao!"

To insure I don't take a misstep, my eyes have been on my feet this entire time. But when I follow the sound of the voice, I am surprised when I look down. Below me, scattered on the jetty's boulders are a group of teenagers, Delia among them. In the time it's taken me to get here, Delia has already situated herself, laying out her beach towel on a flat-topped boulder.

"Here." The boy, who'd first said hello, extends his hand and helps me down. Whoever this boy is, I will forever be grateful to him.

The only problem is, when I take his hand and step down, I misjudge the distance and fall right into him.

While I am embarrassed and eager to get around him, the boy remains in my path, his smile so wide, his gums shine pink.

Delia, now stripped down to her bikini, yells at the boy. "Marco! Stop being so pathetic! Let Anna pass!"

The smile on Marco's face falls, and like a small child, he drifts off to another rock and sulks.

The huge boulders that make up the jetty were never intended to be a place for sunbathing. It's as if a giant, tantrumming baby has taken her blocks and thrown them haphazardly on the ground. As I step from rock to rock, making my way to Delia, I try not to think of what might happen if I slip down into the gaps, and get sucked under.

Somehow, I arrive at Delia's little camp with all my limbs still intact. Whether it is intentional, there's enough space next to her for me to place my towel.

Delia introduces me to the others. "That is Patrizia and Stefano," she says, indicating a cute couple, who share one towel. Patrizia and Stefano have their legs pretzeled together, making for some interesting tan lines, I think.

When I say hello, the two of them acknowledge me with little interest. Not that I blame them. When you've found your other half, what need is there for anyone else?

"You already met my idiot brother," Delia says.

Marco, who's still sulking, frowns deeply.

Delia extends herself on her towel, closes her eyes, and tilts her face up. A satisfied sigh whooshes through her nose. Even when she is fully dressed, Delia's clothes have their work cut out for them, but the two triangles of fabric making up her bikini top, are an engineering miracle.

Patrizia sees me staring at Delia and whispers something in Stefano's ear. I quickly look away.

Delia's bathing suit isn't the only one leaving little to the imagination. Patrizia also wears a two-piece, while both boys sport skimpy Speedos. Reluctantly, I pull off the large, gauzy tent I'm hiding under and reveal the ruffled one-piece number I'd bought for my trip. When it comes to my least favorite things to do, bathing suit shopping and going to the dentist top the list.

I quickly drop belly side down onto my towel. Even in this position, with the sound of the waves echoing in my ears, I can still hear Patrizia giggle. It would be easy to assume that her laughter was due to something Stefano had said or done to her. But somehow I doubt it.

I shut my eyes and squeeze back the tears. Even if Patrizia's laughter has nothing to do with me, it all feels personal.

The black rocks, which have been soaking in the sun, are heat conductors. After a couple of minutes, the delicious warmth radiates through my beach towel. The sun bakes into my flesh, passing deeper into my bones. But when it creeps into the corners where I've kept parts of myself hidden in the cold shadows of my soul, I resist.

My eyes shoot open. Lying next to her as I am, with my nose a few inches away from Delia's shoulder, I can smell the coconut oil she's rubbed into her skin and see the oily beads of perspiration dotting her skin. My heart races and a pleasing warmth that has nothing to do with the sun climbs up between my legs. Even Melissa George has never created this much commotion inside of me.

The shame creeps back. I know there are women like this. Women who are attracted to and love other women. But women like this don't come from the places and the families that I come from. At least, they know better than to live with their shame publicly.

I close my eyes and do my best to fight off this feeling. I am thankful for the bit of distraction when Stefano yells, "O! Roma!"

I assume Stefano's sudden burst of enthusiasm for Rome has something to do with his favorite soccer team. But, when I lift my head up, I notice Stefano is looking toward the sea.

A broad-shouldered boy with a hard, muscular chest, pushes himself up onto the rocks. The droplets of seawater on his tan, toned body create a prismatic effect and he almost glows.

"Who is that?" I ask Delia.

"My cousin," she says.

"And his name is Roma? Like the city?" I say.

Delia chuckles. "No, Rome is where he lives. His real name is Marco, like my brother. But because most of the men in my family are named for my grandfather, Marco, we call this Marco, Roma. That way we don't confuse him with my brother."

As if Delia's brother Marco, who was as thin as a sapling, could ever be confused with this muscular, chiseled-jawed specimen. Roma climbs his way up the rocks. He looks like a rare, mythical beast.

Roma's magnetism is not only obvious to me. Even Stefano has untwined himself from his precious Patrizia and gotten up to greet the god from Rome.

Delia turns to me, which causes her bathing suit to gape open a little bit. "You like him? Don't you?" she says. It's less of a question and more of a judgement.

No normal girl in her right mind would ever say no, but saying yes doesn't feel right either. So, I land on saying nothing.

Somehow my silence is interpreted by Delia as collusion. "Good! I will help you get him!"

Get him? A sense of familiar dread bubbles up inside of me. This is Jack Bennett all over again.

"Yes, I'll teach you," Delia says.

While the warmth I'd felt a moment ago had felt wrong, this feels wrong too, but in a different way.

I try to get out of it by making a joke. "You know, Delia. Getting a boy isn't like learning to drive a car. You can't just teach someone how to do it," I argue.

Delia, however, has a quick rebuttal waiting for me. "It is exactly like driving a car. The woman steers and the car, which is the boy, goes wherever she tells him to go."

47

Delia laughs, and I am mesmerized. But not by Roma.

"What do you say? Do you want to steer the car?" Delia asks.

Shrugging is all I can manage for an answer.

Delia goes back to sunning herself, while I keep my eyes on the water.

8.

Delia again takes the role of leader. Marco and I walk behind her on the way home for lunch. For now, it appears as if Marco has traded in his humiliation for anger. Because every time a cute boy on a scooter passes. Delia makes a point to flirt and wave.

"Control yourself! Don't you see the spectacle you're making of yourself?" Marco shouts at his sister.

"Fuck off! I already have one father!" Delia says, waving at another boy.

Next to me, Marco groans, while my eyes remain fixed on Delia. Every time a boy goes by and beeps, my heart skips a jealous beat.

Another boy goes by and makes a lewd gesture at Delia with his tongue. This is too much for Marco, who finds a rock and kicks it. He misses and, instead, stubs his own toe.

We arrive at my aunt's house, but before we go our separate ways, Delia leans in and whispers in my ear. "We'll start your lessons soon," she says with a wink.

Butterfly Summer

The faint tickle of Delia's breath is still on my ear when I walk into the house and find my aunt standing in the foyer. She is peering down into the open cistern, which is located between the front door and the bottom of the stairs.

Back home, there is a water tank in our basement, which is connected to a pipe that connects to the main that runs up and down our street. Ischia doesn't have a series of pipes like that. The houses here have cisterns, which are big underground tanks that collect the rainwater that is then used for laundering clothes, taking showers and flushing toilets.

I come to stand next to my aunt, who doesn't react to my presence.

"What are you doing?" I ask as I, too, peer into the dark hole in the ground. The cistern is murky, and the lack of light makes it impossible to calculate how deep it goes.

"Don't you smell it?" she says, her voice almost accusatory.

I lean over and take a sniff. Other than the damp odor, I smell nothing unusual.

"It seems fine to me," I say.

Rather than help, my answer only seems to irritate my aunt even more.

"Are you sure? Smell it again," she says.

Whether my aunt is on to something or it's just my desire to please her, I take another whiff. This time, I think I do smell something. "Yes, maybe," I say.

An expression I can't quite pinpoint crosses my aunt's face. "Help me put the lid back," she says, gruffly.

The lid is made of wood. The two of us take a side and awkwardly juggle it into place.

"How did you take this off by yourself?" I say.

As we drop the lid in place, my aunt doesn't answer. Her mind seems stuck on something else.

Later, as I set the table for lunch, my aunt calls out to me from the kitchen. "Set an extra spot. Nennella is eating with us."

It's been a week and half since I last saw that pinch-faced witch. Reluctantly, I add another fork and knife to the table.

When Nennella arrives, she surprises me. She is unusually friendly and chatty, not at all like the woman who'd met me in Rome.

"Ciao, *bella*," she says, when I open the door to let her in. Today, she is dressed in all white, and her hair is brushed in loose waves around her face, giving it a less angular, less harsh appearance. Maybe her outfit is a sign that she's been to church and done penance for her sins. This is the only explanation I have for how nice she is acting now.

Nennella is carrying a dome-shaped package, which she now hands me. The package is wrapped in pink paper and tied with a bow. A small sticker on the paper indicates it's from one of the best pastry shops on the island.

"Put these in the refrigerator before the cream spoils," she says.

The sugary scent drifting out from the paper smells heavenly. *"Grazie per i dolci,"* I say, thanking Nennella for the sweets.

"Brava! Your Italian is improving, I see," Nennella says.

Whatever the reason for her mood change, I decide that I will also try to be nicer.

My aunt emerges from the kitchen, the two of them greeting each other warmly.

"Mamma mia, Maria. For the love of God, please open some windows," Nennella begs.

My aunt does something surprising. She pulls open one of the floor-to-ceiling shutters. In a matter of minutes, the stale air rushes out and is replaced by the fresh sea air. The fresh air lifts our moods, which follows us into the kitchen.

In the kitchen, my aunt allows me to help her prepare the *bracciole* as Nennella sits in my aunt's chair, regaling us with all the latest gossip.

"Did you hear about Sara and Renzo?" Nennella says, as my aunt shows me how to pound the thin layers of beef first before stuffing them with cheese and parsley.

"No. What?" my aunt says, as she rolls the meat and secures the bundles with a thin string.

I place the bundles in a sauce pan of hot oil. The frying meat smells delicious, made more so by the fresh breeze wafting in from the sea.

"The principal found them in the supply closet together. They weren't exactly looking for pencils," Nennella says.

"*Davvero*? Really?" my aunt says, interested in hearing more.

When Nennella relays more of the sordid details about the two teachers, my aunt's eyes get wider, and she even laughs. While it may come at the cost of someone else's reputation, it's nice to see my aunt enjoying herself.

Once everything is cooked, the three of us carry the platters of meat and the accompanying pasta into the living room.

"Thank you for a wonderful lunch," Nennella says to my aunt, after we have eaten every morsel from our plates.

"It helps to not have all that commotion out there," my aunt says, gesturing in the direction of Signor Chiachiaron's gas station. Every day from one to four o'clock in the afternoon, Signor Chiachiaron, like many of the other stores on the corso, closes for lunch. While I don't usually mind the liveliness that circles Signor Chiachiaron, today's lunch is particularly nice because my aunt seems more peaceful.

"Anna, go get the pastries Nennella brought," my aunt says.

I make my way toward the kitchen. While there's still so much that needs to be sorted out inside of me, the last couple of hours have left me lighter, not as bogged down.

When I open the refrigerator to get the pastries, I see that the lid on the box holding the vials is open. While I'm still not sure what the yellow liquid is for, it's become my habit to count the vials each morning when I get the apricot marmalade for my breakfast. Each day, one of the vials is gone, but now there are two missing.

When I return with the pastries, Nennella is in the thick of telling my aunt another story.

"Do you know how long I stood at that bus stop?" Nennella says. "And not one man stopped to ask if I needed a ride." Nennella's complaints, I realize, have nothing to do with good manners.

I place the pastries on the table, anticipating the something sweet to come. But, when I look at my aunt, the flat expression on her face has returned. Evidently, Nennella's latest story is not holding my aunt's interest in the same way the story about the two teachers had.

A burst of familiar noise erupts outside, just as I undo the knot on the string. I glance at the clock. Four o'clock. Time for Signore Chiachiaron's station to get back to action.

Nennella continues with her laments about how men these days have no manners as my aunt picks up the string and begins wrapping it around her finger. She wraps it so tight that her finger turns blue.

Outside, someone lays on their horn a little longer than usual.

"*Basta!*" my aunt says when she's had enough. With the string still wrapped around her finger, she bolts out of her chair and rushes down the stairs.

Nennella throws her hands up in frustration. "Mareee!" she yells, as she starts to follow my aunt.

"What's going on?" I say, joining Nennella on the stairs.

"The same old shit! That's what's going on," Nennella says.

By the time Nennella and I are outside, my aunt is already across the road, yelling at Signore Chiachiaron at the top of her lungs. "It's not enough that you poison my water, but you have to drive me crazy with all your noise too!" she yells directly into Signore Chiachiaron's face.

Rather than yell back, Signore Chiachiaron stands there, patiently taking my aunt's assault.

Nennella and I make our way in between the now growing traffic jam. "Why is she doing this?" I ask Nennella.

"Because she is crazy! That's why!"

While Nennella has proven to be a bit overdramatic, I can't deny my aunt's bristly moods. Not to mention the mysterious yellow vials.

Nennella weaves through the cars, but I shrink back. As Nennella tugs on my aunt's arm, urging her to go back home, people around me say things under their breath about my aunt. A few even laugh. An uncomfortable feeling worms its way down my spine. Not only am I embarrassed for my aunt, but seeing someone I am so closely related to acting in such a way makes me think about my own dark thoughts that keep me up at night.

My aunt finally relents. As Nennella steers my aunt back to her house, for a brief moment, I lock eyes with Signore Chiachiaron. Instead of anger, I read his expression as unquestionably sympathetic. Somehow, this makes everything even worse.

9.

"**B**uongiorno," my aunt says when I enter the kitchen the next morning. The windows are back to being shut, and the rising temperature outside has turned the house back to a sweat box.

"Buongiorno," I say back, taking my spot at the kitchen table.

This morning, my aunt's hair is a limp mop of curls. As she stands at the stove, waiting patiently for the silver coffee pot to spit out the licorice-colored coffee she drinks every morning, she acts as if the scene she created at the gas station the day before never happened.

I, instead, have not been able to push the previous day's events out of my mind. Why had my aunt acted the way she had? Was there some truth to what Nennella had said? Was my aunt really crazy? I'd heard that mental illness was something that ran in families. So, my own constant questioning of myself? Was this a sign of my own imbalance?

My aunt carries her little coffee cup to her seat, across from me. The pastries Nennella had brought, which had gone uneaten, now sit in a box next to the closed window. We each select one. Rather than talking, we keep our mouths busy with the soggy treats.

I think about asking my aunt about the vials of yellow liquid. But something I've learned is that it's easier to avoid knowing something. Because, once the truth is told, a decision has to be made. And whether it concerns my aunt or me, it's not a decision I want to make. At least for now.

This morning, Delia is not the first to arrive. Instead, it is Giovanni, with Arturo behind him like an eager puppy.

Since my aunt is still in the kitchen when the two boys arrive, it gives Giovanni license to throw his books on the table and show his true colors. "If I have to sit in this heat for one more day, my balls are going to shrivel up and turn into prunes!" Giovanni complains loudly.

Giovanni's lament touches a nerve in me. After my aunt's assault on poor Signore Chiachiaron, I'm beginning to wonder what the real reason is behind my aunt's desire to shut the world out.

Most boys would jump on the bandwagon. Not Arturo. Instead of chiming in, Arturo's face turns red at the mention of pruney balls.

"At least I have balls, tuna breath," Giovanni says to Arturo, who buries his head in his book.

Poor Arturo. Why is he so desperate for Giovanni's approval? If it wasn't for the fact that I'm waiting for the sound of the door downstairs to open, I would reach out and smack Giovanni in the face.

Where is Delia? And why is she late? Has she already forgotten about me?

When the door finally does bang open, and I hear the sound of Delia's sandals flapping against the marble stairs, I can finally breathe.

Delia emerges at the top of the steps just as my aunt enters the living room.

"You're late," my aunt tells her.

"I'm sorry, Professoressa," Delia says, as she slides into the chair next to me. "Shall I do the next chapter?" My aunt simply nods, and Delia gets down to business.

And so do I. The two of us seem to have come to a silent agreement. At the table, we will work speedily and efficiently. But even as I translate more of Marcovaldo's story, the hairs on my arms sense how close Delia is to me. Like tiny divining rods, they rise up, seeking what they are looking for.

Like the day before, Delia is the first one to finish. And in a repeat of yesterday, she gets a perfect score.

My aunt has an accordion file where she keeps everyone's summer work. Each section has a tab with each student's name written on the tab. Oddly, she's even made a tab with my name on it.

Arturo and I finish at the same time. Giovanni grumbles. He hates being last. So much so, he breaks the point of his pencil from leaning too hard.

Delia and I gather our beach bags. My aunt gives Arturo permission to go too. Instead, he drifts to my aunt's bookcase. "Professoressa, is this the book you were telling me about? Do you mind if I sit here and read awhile?" Arturo asks my aunt.

"Why don't you bring it home with you?" my aunt says.

"It's kind of heavy. I much rather read it here," Arturo says.

"Do as you like," my aunt says.

As Arturo sits back down, Giovanni rolls his eyes.

Before I can figure out why Arturo would choose to spend another minute in this sweltering prison, Delia says, "Let's go."

Once we are outside, the air is gloriously cool.

"Aren't we going to the port to swim?" I say, when I realize that Delia is pulling me in the opposite direction than the day before.

"Swim? Is that what you call what you did?" Delia says, her tone a bit mocking.

True. Without any sense of how deep the water was, I'd spent the day before baking in the sun, while the rest of them had gone swimming.

"No, today, we're going to take a walk and see where that leads," Delia says.

But that day at the cemetery proves that Delia isn't one to leave things up to chance.

As she walks, her arms swing with a steady certainty. This thrills me, but it also scares me. In the short time I've known Delia, in my heart, I know I will follow her wherever she leads me.

On the way to wherever we are going, we pass a shop that sells yarn, knitting needles, crochet hooks, and books with instructions to make all types of woven creations. A small group of old women sit in the shade on chairs, all of them with fingers flying as they loop yarn around their crochet hooks. The women have monopolized a good portion of the sidewalk and Delia and I are forced to step into the street to get around them. As we pass, one of the old women looks up from her handywork and, with a judgmental scowl directed at Delia, mumbles something to the other ladies.

When we've passed, I say to Delia. "Do you know them?"

"Ignore those witches. They think they know everything about everyone," Delia says, picking up her pace.

We get to the piazza. On the flat edge of the fountain I passed the first day I arrived, two elderly men sit talking. Both of them are loud, their hands flying to accentuate their points. The only time the men stop talking is when an attractive woman walks by. Beyond the fountain, at the far end of the piazza, sits the taxi depot. Next to the taxis are two kiosks. One sells magazines and newspapers. Some of the newspapers are draped over long wooden poles, their pages fluttering whenever they are brushed by a breeze. The other kiosk sells plastic beach toys, pails and shovels, as well as water-wings, and life preservers. There's even a giant blow-up raft in the shape of a big red crab tied to the roof of the kiosk.

All of this, even the row of payphones marked up with graffiti, feels somehow magical with Delia next to me.

Beyond the phones, at the opposite end of the piazza sits the popular café where Nennella bought her ill-fated pastries. While there are other bars on the island, none is more popular or fancier than this café Its main entrance has a curved staircase leading up to a patio where deep-pocketed tourists are willing to pay extra money for waiter service. Seats with deep-cushioned chairs line the patio so the customers can eat their ice cream or sip on a drink while Gino, the piano player, sings Neapolitan songs, along with more modern tunes.

An ice cream or something cold to drink would be perfect on the hot day, but Delia avoids the main staircase and walks toward another set of stairs leading to the lower level of the bar.

Down the stairs, beyond a couple of potted palms, there is a door. The room we enter is narrow, with a row of white, plastic chairs pushed up against one of the walls and some arcade games. But when I see who is standing at the far end of the room, I realize that this day has nothing to do with Delia and I, and my heart sinks.

Delia greets Roma and Marco. "Ciao *ragazzi!*" she says.

Roma doesn't say a word. He's too engrossed in the foosball game he and Marco are playing.

But when Marco sees me, he smiles shyly and says, "Ciao."

This tiny lapse in his attention is just what Roma needs to gain an advantage. Seeing an opening, he lines up the tiny plastic soccer players on his team and gives the metal bars a quick spin. And *fwack!*

"*Porcamiseria!*" Marco curses.

Roma slaps Marco hard on the back of the head and laughs. He looks at me and smiles, his cigarette-stained teeth now visible to me for the first time. His teeth are the same yellow as Jack Bennett's shorts. Something inside of me shrivels. But because this isn't the place to give myself away, I smile back.

My pretend interest has a ripple effect. Marco goes and sits on a stool in the corner where he starts picking his cuticles. Clearly, he is jealous and, for this, I feel bad for him. Delia, on the other hand, is delighted. In her mind, she's seen a spark between her cousin and I.

"Roma, let's go smoke. Anna, you come too," she says, ready to fan the imaginary flame.

There is another door on the back wall. The three of us exit the arcade, leaving poor Marco by himself.

The door leads to a small alcove, where someone's stacked another pile of plastic chairs. The space is tight, leaving a small space for us to stand hip-to-hip. From the number of cigarette butts littering the ground, it's clear we aren't the only ones who've used this spot for this purpose.

Roma takes a pack of cigarettes from his shirt pocket

and, with a pinky nail that's an inch longer than the rest of his nails, he slices along the red line, uncoiling the cellophane. The smell of cigarette smoke lingering in the air, coupled with the sight of Roma's ugly nail, erases any meager attraction I had for him,

The cellophane is discarded, added to the rest of the debris on the ground. Roma shakes the pack, loosening the cigarettes. As he extends his hand to offer me one, he brushes my left breast ever so slightly.

Instinctively, I take a step back. Roma smirks, proving he'd done it on purpose, and he enjoyed watching me squirm.

When I hesitate at his offer, Roma sounds incredulous. "You don't smoke?"

While cigarettes might not be drugs, I've always thought them filthy. As Nancy Reagan's T.V. campaign and its ubiquitous saying *just say no* rings in my ears, Delia cocks her head and shoots me a look. What Roma thinks of me, isn't important. Like Jack Bennett, it never was. But Delia on the other hand? Hers is the opinion that matters most to me. So, I pull a cigarette out of the pack and Delia follows suit.

I'm grateful when Roma lights Delia's cigarette first. It gives me a chance to study the way she closes her lips and pulls in the smoke. Her nostrils flare a bit, releasing the smoke through her nose. I've seen actresses in old black and white movies flare their nostrils in just the same way, but never has it looked so captivating.

I try my best to repeat Delia's actions, but, once I draw in the smoke, it tickles my throat.

I cough so hard, my eyes tear up. A little bit of snot even escapes my nose. To make matters worse, Roma starts laughing at me. But this time, as the shame at the tennis courts is repeated, I am close to grabbing Roma by the shirt and shoving him into the bushes. However, before I can defend myself, Delia does it for me. But she does it in a surprising way.

"You were conned, Roma," Delia says.

Roma's laughter immediately dries up. He squares his shoulders, but I can tell that Delia has said something that offends him. "What do you mean?" he says.

"You won these in a game, didn't you?" Delia says.

Roma shrugs but doesn't seem to want to openly admit to the truth.

"I knew it. Those boys gave you crap cigarettes," she says. To make her point further, Delia throws her cigarette on the ground.

"Oh, like you're some expert?" Roma says, his ego-obviously bruised.

"I may not be the expert, but Anna is," Delia says.

I appreciate that Delia is sticking up for me, but secretly I pray that I won't be called out to prove my expertise.

"Tell him, Anna," Delia says to me. "Tell him how when you're in America, you only smoke Marlboro."

"Yes. Only Marlboros," I say, hoping Roma doesn't pick up on the slight quiver in my voice.

"See," Delia says, using the same tag team method she'd used at the cemetery.

Roma tips back on his feet a bit, a sign that Delia's knocked his confidence off balance.

To prove to Delia that she can count on me to back her up, I repeat a motion I've also seen in movies. I drop my cigarette on the floor and give it a little twist with the bottom of my sandal.

Roma tries to save face. After a few more quick puffs he flicks the remainder of his cigarette into a nearby hedge. His perfectly chiseled face is now marred with disgust, but all I care about is Delia's approving smile when she looks at me.

10.

Since I got here, a transistor radio has sat on top of my aunt's refrigerator, the cord wrapped around it. For my aunt, music seems to be an irritation. Every time I pop a cassette into my Walkman, she looks at me and frowns, even with my headphones in and the volume on low. So, the next morning, when I walk into the kitchen, I'm surprised to find that the radio has been pulled down from its resting spot. My aunt, who is spreading some marmalade onto a piece of toast, is humming along to a song on the radio.

Avrai sorrisi sul tuo viso come un sole d'Agosto . . . You'll have smiles on your face like the August sun.

I don't know what surprises me more: my aunt's unusually light mood or the fact that I can figure out the lyrics with no problem.

"Buongiorno," I say, as I greet my aunt.

Butterfly Summer

"Buongiorno," she says back.

As she places the toast on two plates – one for her and one for me – I go to the refrigerator for a drink. Since that day when I first met Delia, I'd lost the taste for milk. Delia is right. Milk is for babies. And it is time for me to grow up.

As I go to pull out the carton of peach juice, I'd asked my aunt to add to her daily grocery list, I do a quick calculation. Seven vials. The same number as the day before.

I've struggled with whether to tell my parents about the whole Signore Chiachiaron incident. If my aunt is sick in some way, wouldn't they want to know?

My aunt continues to sing. "*Quando sei innamorato, tuo sorriso brilla come le stelle.* "When you're in love, your smile shines bright like the stars."

At least for now, there seems to be no need to say anything to my parents.

The morning feels lighter for other reasons. After the whole cigarette incident with Roma, Delia's opinion of him seemed to have shifted.

"He's always thought too highly of himself, because he lives in Rome," she'd said on the walk back home. "I thought it was Marco just being jealous, but he said Roma puts us all down."

"Puts you down?" I'd asked.

"Me and my whole family," Delia explained. "His father went to school and has an office job, so Roma thinks that makes his family better than ours."

"Working in an office doesn't make someone a better person," I reassured Delia.

"It shouldn't," Delia said, her normal confidence dimming. It was as if the source of all her brightness had suddenly been cut off "I hate how other people get to make the rules," Delia sighed.

64

In that moment, it had taken every ounce of willpower to not squeeze Delia's hand, letting her know that I understood what feeling trapped by other people's rules felt like. But before I could muster up courage, the switch was flipped back, and Delia went back to talking about music and clothes, and the rest of the normal things that are supposed to be the focus of a teenager's life.

I pretended to listen, but this small peek into Delia's vulnerable side, touched something deep in me.

Now, as my aunt and I eat breakfast, the DJ from Radio Kiss Kiss spins records.

"I like this song," my aunt says. She taps her foot as if her own teenage years are not as far in the past as one would think.

"I like it too," I say.

What would it be like to have a real conversation I wonder? One where we don't have to hide who we really are?

The words get tangled in my throat. The song we both like plays out. It's time for lessons.

The four of us get to work on our lessons, but with Delia barely a foot away from me, I find it impossible to concentrate. Instead of Marcovaldo and his stupid mushrooms, all I can focus on is the improbable shade of mahogany the sun has turned Delia's skin. Delia is a lefty. She writes with her right hand propping up her head. The curls flow over Delia's shoulder, the tiny, bleached hairs on the back of her neck hypnotizing me.

In an attempt to release myself from this trance, I squeeze my eyes. When I open them, Arturo is looking right at me. A chill spreads through me. A juicy piece of gossip is just what Arturo needs to impress Giovanni. I hold my breath and wait for him to finally be the one to whisper something crass in Giovanni's ear. Whether he is too nice or doesn't understand what he's just seen, Arturo doesn't sacrifice me. He simply returns to the extra work my aunt gave him, since he's already done with his regular schoolwork.

The door to my aunt's house closes and the day's adventure is ready for us. The warmth of the sun melts into my body. I'm ready to shed the costume I feel I need to wear whenever I am around my aunt. I remind myself that I need to temper my excitement. What if it had been Giovanni, not Arturo, who'd noticed me staring longingly at the back of Delia's neck? What then? The dream of a free and unfettered summer, away from judgmental eyes, I now realize is an unrealistic one. If anything, Ischia's rumor mill makes my high school rumor mill look like a bunch of amateurs.

"Where to today?" I ask Delia. On the outside, I maintain a calm exterior. On the inside, I am giddy about the prospect of spending another day together.

"You'll see," she says, the one side of her mouth curling up in a mysterious smile.

Though Delia's surprises make me nervous, on account they're not always in line with what I want, my heart races when Delia cloaks something in mystery. Delia makes me feel like a little kid on Christmas morning. It's in this sense that anything is possible that leaves me wanting more of her.

Since the day my aunt rushed at him, and mainly due to my own embarrassment over the incident, I've avoided making eye contact with Signore Chiachiaron. But now, as there is no way to avoid it, Signore Chiachiaron lifts his head and waves to us.

"Ciao, Signore!" Delia calls out to him.

"Ciao, Delia! Give my regards to your parents," Signore Chiachiaron says.

Delia makes a promise to do just that, which make me feel even more awkward about my aunt's scene.

As we head along the corso, Delia says, "I saw the way Roma brushed up against you when he handed you the cigarettes. He really does likes you, you know?"

Her remarks punch me in the gut and rob me of my breath. After the cigarette fiasco and her own criticism of her cousin, I was sure she'd given up wanting to play matchmaker. Apparently, I am wrong.

Delia takes a turn, down a narrow lane. It's a road we've never taken before. My feet follow her blindly, but it's as if I've left a piece of me back on the corso. Why did Delia stand up for me against Roma with the intention of throwing me back to the wolf again? With each step, it is becoming increasingly more obvious to me that I've misread Delia. I am the pathetic American niece of Delia's teacher, a teacher she doesn't even particularly like or admire. My sole purpose is for her amusement. Nothing else. And once she discovers I'm not even good for that? Then what?

We come to a storefront. Other than the curled poster of Sophia Loren that hangs in the window, the store doesn't have a sign. A curtain of long beads hangs in the entryway of the shop. In the time we stand there, the beads hang limply and don't move. No one goes into the shop nor do they exit.

"What you need is a complete makeover," Delia says.

Ironically, the one reason I'd come here this summer was to transform myself. Or, at the very least, to figure out a way for other people to view me in a slightly more palatable way. But Delia's declaration is so blunt it stings, only reconfirming everything I've always hated about myself.

Delia fingers my ponytail. "This hair," she says.

Even though her tone is less than complimentary, and I now see there's nothing personal behind the gesture, my body can't help but react to her touch. My cheeks flush.

"Eh. No worries. Donatella is a genius. She'll figure it out."

Delia approaches the shop and pushes the beads aside. The assumption is that I will just follow her as I always do, but this time, a tiny bit of defiance stirs in me and I don't move.

A second later, the beads part and Delia pokes her head out. "*O*! What are you waiting for?"

What *am* I waiting for? Without an answer, the defiance in me has nothing to fuel it.

Calling the shop a beauty salon would be a major overstatement. One barber chair, its vinyl seat cracked and showing its stuffing, occupies the middle of the room. A couple more posters, similar to the one in the window, hang on the walls, but there's little else to inspire confidence in a client hoping to walk out feeling like a million bucks.

"Donatella! Wooohooo!" Delia calls out.

More beads hang over a doorway leading to the back of the shop. The beads swing out and a girl appears. "Bella!" Donatella shrieks as she comes to greet Delia. The two of them share a double-air kiss on the cheek.

Donatella's style is in a completely different class than my usual shapeless t-shirts and cut-offs. Donatella is wearing a black, Rolling Stones concert T-shirt, its neckline strategically cut, allowing for it to fall low on one shoulder. Her jeans are so tight they look painted on, and her short, cropped hair looks like it's been cut with a razor blade, the tips dyed a light pink color. Does Delia actually have faith in this girl?

Delia explains to Donatella that she wants Donatella to cut my hair. At least, this is what I think she is telling her. The two girls are talking in rapid-fire Neapolitan, and I'm only able to pick up a few words here and there. There is one word that stands out.

Desperate.

Even without any real context to wrap it around, it feels safe to assume that the desperate one in this moment is me.

There are no other hairdressers or even clients. There isn't even a mirror hanging on the wall. What kind of place is this? Have I totally misjudged Delia? Like Melissa George, have I focused too much on how attracted I am to Delia, rather than her as a person?

Donatella seems confident that she can help me and, before I know it, she's wrapped a black cape around my neck and pushed me into the chair.

As Donatella starts attacking my hair with scissors, the two girls continue their conversation. I am just the disembodied head sitting in the squeaky chair.

The last time I trusted someone to make a decision on my hair, I was eight. My mother thinking my hair would look great in a poodle cut like hers, took me to her stylist. But even the extra lollipops afterward did nothing to help me feel better.

This time it's worse. I'd trusted Delia for a different reason. As tufts of my hair become airborne and land on the floor, this feels like a betrayal.

Donatella continues cutting. Delia watches each snip, but her expression gives nothing away.

Does she like it? And does she see a prettier, happier, better version of me?

The process doesn't end with the cutting. There's more. Donatella applies a humungous glob of something sticky to my wet hair. She fires up the air dryer and proceeds to knead, mold, and sculpt. If Michelangelo was alive today, surely he'd be working with hair instead of marble.

Donatella performs her work with strength and determination. Surely, it is this shared character traits that make Delia and Donatella friends. It's also another reason why Delia would never be able to consider me as something more than just a project.

When Donatella is done, she says, "I'll be right back."

Delia looks at me, her expression unreadable.

When Donatella returns, she's holding a hand mirror, but she waits before handing it to me. "What do you think?" she says, to Delia, instead of me.

Delia's expression goes from unreadable to ecstatic. "Donatella, it's wonderful!" she says.

This whole time I've been trying to convince myself that Delia's opinion doesn't matter when, in reality, it is all I care about.

I take the mirror from Donatella so I can assess it myself.

"What do you think?" she asks.

The reflection mirrored back catches me off guard. Donatella has performed a minor miracle! The lank waves being held up by a Scrunchie this entire time, now fall in perfect layers around my face.

Delia takes a closer look. "*Fantastica*," she says.

I agree. I look great! What strikes me most is that Delia, imagining how fantastic my hair could look, had been able to express her vision to Donatella. It is as if Delia knew that the girl in the mirror had been there all along.

Because Delia has displayed faith in me, I forgive her again, just as I'd done when she called me a baby in my aunt's kitchen or accused me of being too scared to jump from the jetty. Forgiveness is, I believe, what you do for a person you have feelings for. And I still want to believe that, if I just give her some time, Delia will discover that she has feelings for me too.

We are a fair distance from the beauty shop when a thought occurs to me. "Oh, no! I forgot to pay Donatella!"

Delia waves her hand. "You don't need to pay her. The girl isn't even a real hairdresser."

"What do you mean not real?"

"She doesn't even have a cosmetology license. The salon belonged to Massimo, but he's in Milan now."

I stop in the middle of the lane. "What are you talking about?"

Delia sighs, as if an explanation isn't really necessary. "Donatella and her parents live next door. They own the space and rent it out. Now that it's empty, Donatella likes to play beauty shop."

I run my hand through my hair. Knowing the truth makes me suddenly conscious of all the imperfections.

"You're angry," Delia says.

Delia has been pushy about other things, but this time feels even more personal.

"No," I say, shaking my head. I want to please her so badly that I allow her the satisfaction while denying my own. Still, it hurts and tears form in my eyes.

I catch glimpses of myself in the storefront windows that we pass. The waves Donatella had so carefully molded are already beginning to lose their shape and my hair is starting to frizz. The impracticality of the style is starting to show and confirms what I already know about myself. Being pretty is something for other girls. Not me.

Delia does something unexpected. She tugs lightly at one of the waves, flipping it. "It really does look good," she says.

The tears recede. I feel whole again.

Delia's approval and no one else's is all that I need.

"Come on. Let's take a walk around the piazza," Delia suggests.

I see what she's doing. This time of day, there are always a bunch of boys parked outside the Bar Italia. How can I make Delia understand that I don't want to parade myself around like a show dog to catch a boy's attention?

"Ouch," I say, feigning a little limp.

"Are you okay?" Delia says.

"It's a blister, I think. Can we sit by the fountain? Maybe I can cool my feet off in the water," I say.

I am relieved when Delia doesn't fight me on the idea.

Delia and I take the place that the two elderly men had occupied the day before. We remove our flip-flops, then turn on the edge to face the spouting center. Together we dip our feet in the water. The shock of the cold water makes me shiver, as does the pleasure from sitting next to Delia.

Even though I tried to avoid them, from where we are sitting, we have an unobstructed view of Bar Italia, and the group of teenaged boys congregated outside.

As Delia splashes her feet in the water, all of her attention is laser-focused on the boys. Pretending to have a blister wasn't enough. I need to do something else to steer Delia's attention toward me.

As I work out a plan to pretend a tiny leaf or a speck of dirt has landed on Delia's cheek, giving me just cause to move her face so that she can finally *see* me, Delia says something completely unexpected.

"Useless. All of them. They want us to chase them, but, really, what are we chasing? Nothing. We'd be better without them," Delia says, referring back to the boys.

While Delia had expressed how stupid she thought her cousin Roma was, and it was pretty obvious how she felt about her brother, I am shocked to hear what she thinks about other boys. Shocked but happy. Does this mean that Delia is like me?

I am about to ask Delia if she truly believes that all boys are useless, when she leans forward and dips her hand in the water. At first, I think she is reaching for some of the coins that people have thrown into the fountain. But she opens the palm of her hand and reveals to me that what she's scooped up is an oblong-shaped pod. The walls of the pod are paper-thin, almost translucent.

She holds it up for me to see it better. "Do you see its wings?"

What I'd first assumed was a plant pod, I see is a butterfly cocoon. With my eyes, I trace the outline of the butterfly's curled wings.

Delia raises the pod to the level of her own eyes.

"Why is it stuck in there?" I ask.

"Some things never get a chance to live, I suppose," Delia says. There's a strange tension in Delia's voice as she continues to stare at the tiny, stuck creature.

I want to touch Delia's cheek and force her to look at me, but, like always, I lose my nerve.

Delia shakes her head. "Time to go," she says, without bothering to check her watch. She places her hand back in the water, releasing the cocoon back to its watery grave.

11.

Delia doesn't say much on our way back. Even when a boy on a scooter beeps at us, vying for our attention, she ignores him.

It's not until Signore Chiachiaron's station comes into view that Delia finally says to me, "I'm glad you came to Italy this summer, Anna. People here are very close-minded, but you? I think you are different."

Up until this point, different has only meant bad and shameful things. In the late 1800's an earthquake hit Ischia. The same fault line that caused the earth to shake runs under our feet now but has nothing to do with the trembling I feel in my body. Even if I had the courage to tell Delia how I feel about her, we've come to my aunt's house where a very curious Signore Chiachiaron has his eyes trained on us.

As I head up the stairs, I feel light. The day spent with Delia has buoyed my soul. I can't remember the last time I felt this way. I don't want it to stop. If anything, I want to build upon what seems to be a promising start between the two of us.

The minute my aunt sees my hair, my good mood is punctured. "Did Delia make you do this?"

My aunt has only been kind to me since I've been here, but I'm tired of towing the line. "Does it matter? I like my hair," I say.

The heat in the house means my aunt is always in a constant state of perspiration, but my small act of defiance triggers a tiny line of watery beads that bloom along her upper lip.

"Be careful with that girl," my aunt warns me.

Whether it's Delia who has emboldened me or maybe the heat, I stand up straight and say, "You sound just like him, A'zi."

The two of us know who *him* is. My comment triggers the resentment my aunt has toward my father. It evokes a meanness in her that is so different than her usual passivity. "Yes. And I'll call *him* right now, Anna. I'm sure Nennella will have no problem bringing you back to Rome early."

My aunt means it, and I quickly back down. "Sorry."

"Now go set the table for lunch."

Without another word, I open the drawer by the sink and count out an even amount of forks and spoons. I retrieve a water glass for each of us.

My aunt stands at the stove stirring the pot of minestrone. Who eats hot soup in the middle of July?

"Don't forget the grated cheese," my aunt reminds me.

"*Si*," I say, reaching for the small, lidded dish that holds the cheese. I perform my role meticulously. On the surface, it looks as if I've settled back into my usual compliant self, but inside, I am quietly protesting. Genetic makeup aside, I refuse to wall myself off from life the way she does.

Butterfly Summer

The next day when Delia and I arrive at the jetty, neither Roma nor Marco are there.

"My uncle went back home for a couple of days and he took my cousin with him, " Delia explains. Because her own brother's presence matters less to her, Delia doesn't bother explaining his whereabouts.

So, with the exception of Patrizia and Stefano who are back to their pretzel-position, it is just Delia and I. As we've done every other time, we place our towels side by side.

Part of the reason Delia is so tan is due to the oil she rubs into her legs and arms. The oil is the color of warm caramel and it smells what I imagine a spice market in India might smell like. Delia rubs the smell of India onto her arms and legs.

"Rub my shoulders?" Delia says, handing me the bottle of oil.

Delia turns her back. She piles her hair on top of her head and keeps her hands there as she waits for me. My heart is pounding as I work the oil onto her skin. The oil stays on the surface for a few seconds before penetrating Delia's skin. As I make my way to Delia's lower back, she sighs, which triggers a pleasurable, throbbing sensation between my legs.

Behind me Patrizia giggles. For all I know, the girl might not be laughing at me, but rather at something Stefano has said. Either way, I don't want to know. I've decided that tuning out the opinions of others is something I need to practice. And, if I don't want to end up like my aunt, I need to be braver too.

I hand Delia the oil and stand up. "I'm going for a swim," I announce.

As I crabwalk my way down the rocks, to where the sea splashes against the jagged granite, I sense that the three of them are watching and waiting to see if I'll actually do it this time.

When I jump, I forget that, though they're not visible on the surface, the rocks extend out and I stub my toe. But, after the initial pain subsides, the water is glorious. When I feel a bit more trusting, I flatten my back and extend my arms and legs out like a starfish. The water here is so much saltier than the ocean back home making it easier to float.

My ears are submerged, pushing out the rest of the world. The only sound I can hear is the whooshing sound of my heart. Up until now, I've never given my heart much thought. Like a finger or my nose, I've viewed it as just another body part. But now it's as if there's another person living inside of me, and it wants to give me a message.

Before I can make out this message, water sprays over my face and gets up my nose. I open my eyes and there's Delia, treading water right next to me.

"I don't know what you were afraid of," Delia says. She tilts back, and when she lifts her head up, her hair is dripping wet. The sunlight catches the curls, creating a halo of little stars around her head. "You just need to jump in. That's all."

I recognize in Delia's words that this is the exact message my heart was trying to tell me all along.

Butterfly Summer

The two of us swim and splash for a good long while. By the time we climb back up the rocks, Patrizia and Stefano are already gone.

After we dry off, Delia suggests we get an ice cream cone. Even though it's close to lunchtime, I happily follow Delia to the café.

Today, we use the staircase that leads to the upper part of the restaurant. Just before we pass through the main entrance, an older man who sits at one of the paying tables on the patio, tips his head at Delia and says, "Buongiorno."

Delia tips her head politely and we head for the ice cream counter.

The bar has high tables where we stand and eat our ice cream. At least, I am eating my ice cream. Delia's ice cream is beginning to melt because she's too busy staring out toward the patio at the man. He's an ugly beast, with a thick, gray beard that sticks out unevenly from his face. Right now, he is talking so loudly to the waiter that everyone else in the café can also hear.

"Do you know him?" I say, uncomfortable with the way Delia is watching him.

"Everyone in Ischia knows him," Delia says back. "See that car?"

I bend a little and stretch my neck. At the bottom of the café's staircase, parked at the curb, sits a sleek, red convertible. A car like this stands out on an island where the narrow streets and the high price of gas make scooters or small Fiats more sensible options.

"He owns that car," Delia says. "Along with a big villa and the big grocery store in Piazza Bagni where my mother shops," Delia explains.

The man laughs. It's the laugh of a rich man who wants everyone to know that he can easily afford the extra service fee, while the rest of us are forced to eat our ice cream standing up.

It bothers me a lot how Delia is eyeing this man up and down. There's a hunger in her eyes that makes me jealous, but also a little scared because I've been taught that a girl should avoid a man like this.

I want Delia to know that she's so much better than this man, but all I can do is point to her ice cream cone and say, "You're melting,"

Delia looks at the melted mess and frowns. Instead of eating more quickly, she completely gives up, tossing what's left into a nearby trash can.

I am relieved when the man finally tosses some lira on the table and leaves.

That following Sunday, my aunt and I are invited for lunch at Delia's house. Other than meeting her mother at the cemetery and her brother and cousin, I know little about the rest of Delia's family. I like the idea of spending more time with Delia. But being around people who might notice how many times my cheeks flush when I stand close to Delia, or how hard I laugh when she tells a joke, makes me nervous.

Before we leave for Delia's house, my aunt stretches the cord of her black, rotary phone from where it sits on her desk, and places it in the center of the round table.

The phone rings and my aunt twists the cord around her finger. It's a gesture I've seen my father do with the cord of our harvest-gold phone.

"Ciao, Maria!" my father shouts through the phone.

"Ciao," my aunt yells back.

My parents ask me the same exact questions they asked me the previous week. Do I like the food? Am I wearing a hat? Am I minding my aunt, or am I giving her too much trouble?

While my mother is mainly interested in the first two questions, my father is most concerned about the last one.

Usually, I am not too worried about my aunt's answer. This week though I wait for her to mention something about the way I'd defended my choice.

My aunt doesn't say a word. However, she does snitch on me about my haircut.

"Do you like it, Anna?" my mother wants to know.

"Yes," I say, but not with too much enthusiasm since I don't want my aunt to tell my parents that it was Delia's idea and not mine.

My mother's only care is that I am pleased. My father, on the other hand, is happy because I didn't have to pay for it.

Nothing is mentioned regarding my impertinence and the conversation quickly turns to the usual Sunday script.

"How are you feeling, Maria?" my mother asks.

As my aunt launches into her litany of physical complaints – the bursitis in her shoulder, the molar the dentist said might need to be pulled, the prickly, rough patch of skin on her right elbow - I think about the glass vials. That morning, I counted one less than the day before. My aunt's eyelids are becoming heavy as she listens to my father go on and on about the humidity.

From outside, Signore Chiachiaron's voice rises up, his happy chatter managing to squeeze through the slats of the closed shutters. It's such a sharp contrast to my aunt's lack of vitality and overheated existence.

Is this the time to bring up my concerns?

But, as I weigh how to bring it up in the conversation, my mother's egg timer goes off three-thousand miles away.

Our time is up. After another flurry of ciaos, my aunt places the receiver back on its cradle and my chance is lost.

At Delia's house, a long table is set up in the garden. Bees, with hairy legs, buzz over our heads as Delia and I sit in the shade of a pergola. Delia twists the radio dial, searching for her favorite music station. On the other side of the garden, Marco and Delia's father, Carlo, play cards. From time to time, Marco steals glances at me, which I promptly ignore.

Delia continues with the dial, but nothing goes beyond her notice. Not even her brother. Especially not her brother. "Marco likes you," she says. "At night, I hear him flipping around in his bed like a fish looking for air. He's so in love with you he can't sleep."

Most girls are happy when a boy likes them. For me, it's a lot of work. I have to act happy and somewhat grateful for a boy's attention, when the reality is, I rather be invisible to the opposite sex.

To play along, I offer Delia a weak smile, while scratching at a nasty mosquito bite on the back of my leg.

"Oh, don't worry, Anna. Marco knows you're too good for him. He won't try anything. And, if he does, I'll make him very unhappy."

While I wouldn't want Delia to hurt her brother, the idea that she would defend me against his advances makes me feel somewhat special in her eyes. Like Arturo, the tips of my ears get warm.

Butterfly Summer

Delia finally lands on the station she wants. She closes her eyes and starts swaying to the music, the music pouring into her. It is these rare, perfect moments when no one seems to be looking, and it is just Delia and I, that make me the happiest.

Unfortunately, the garden is filled with other people. Aside from Marco and Carlo, Delia's soon-to-be brother-in-law, Paolo, is also at the table. A medical student, Paolo isn't interested in playing cards. Instead, he prefers to read his book.

On the way over here, my aunt gushed. "Paolo has a very good family background, and he is a gifted student. He's above her class," my aunt said, referring to Rosalba, Delia's older sister. "She's lucky to have him."

The idea that one person can have more value than another simply because they are better at school isn't something I agree with. But it's not just my aunt who has this belief. When we first arrived, everyone, even Carlo, Delia's father, bowed down to Paolo, giving his future son-in-law the chair with the cushion, instead of taking it himself.

I look back at Paolo. His narrow nose and delicate, rosebud-shaped lips are a bit too precious in my opinion. The book he is reading has a picture on its cover of a grimacing man, writhing in agony. Compared to Rosalba, who struck me as very sweet when I first met her, Paolo is an overeducated twit.

The radio station Delia likes plays a mix of music in Italian and English. The song that plays now is in English.

"What are they saying?" Delia says, wanting me to translate for her.

The music is too fast and some of the words don't even make sense. "Sorry, my Italian isn't that good," I explain.

"But you understand me when I talk and I understand you," she says.

"That's different," I say.

"How?"

"I don't know. It just is," I say. How do I explain to Delia that when she talks, I'm not only connecting words the way I do when I'm translating Marcovaldo's story. Studying a language is not like studying a person, there are no rules for conjugating a person. But I do know when Delia wrinkles the bridge of her nose, she is bothered, and that when she laughs from her stomach, she finds something stupid or ridiculous. And when her eyes sparkle, it is because something is making her very, very happy. Like now.

Cyndi Lauper comes on the radio.

"Oh! I love this song," Delia says, pulling me up to dance with her.

Delia dances freely, her hips swinging seductively to Cyndi's gravelly voice.

Dancing is just another thing that has always left me feeling uncomfortable, but when Delia grabs my hands and forces me into the rhythm of the song. I give in. And, just like the song says, I start to have fun!

With an expression matching the cover of his book, Paolo screams, "Turn that whore song down!"

The crudeness of the insult, combined with Paolo's baritone voice, which is not a match with his scrawny physique, stops me in my tracks. Delia, on the other hand, takes a step toward the radio and raises the volume. She returns to our makeshift dance floor and, egging me on to follow her, throws her hands in the air and adds even more hip and shoulder action than before.

Marco grumbles something in his father's ear. Carlo, who is dressed in a stained undershirt, yells at his daughter, but the music drowns out his voice.

Delia keeps dancing. "Come on, Anna!" she yells.

83

I make a weak attempt at keeping up, but with everyone's eyes on us, my moves no longer match the beat of the song.

The song winds down just as Rosalba and Delia's mother, Nunzia, come out of the house. The two women wear identical aprons, each one carrying a large bowl. One bowl is heaped with pasta, the other is filled with meat in a rich ragu. The smell of garlic is so strong it overpowers the fragrant honeysuckle bush growing along the fence.

Rosalba is a nervous little squirrel, and she picks up on the tension right away. "What's going on? What did you do?" Rosalba says, glaring at Delia.

"Me? Why do you assume that I am the problem?" Delia says.

"Because you always are," Rosalba says.

From a morning spent in a hot kitchen, Nunzia looks sweaty and tired. "Delia, shut off the radio," she says, her tone clearly annoyed. But when Nunzia speaks to me, her tone switches over to something sweeter. "Anna, Bella, wake up your aunt. Tell her lunch is ready."

On the opposite side of the garden, my aunt is sprawled out on a lounge chair. Soon after we arrived, she hadn't been able to keep her eyes open another minute and fell fast asleep.

"A'zi." I don't speak too loudly, afraid of startling her out of a deep sleep. One of her shoes has fallen off, revealing the seam of her pantyhose that runs along the tip of her toes. This seam, along with how perfectly still my aunt is, reminds me of a plastic doll I once had. When I wasn't playing with that doll, it sat at the bottom of my toy chest, lifeless and unanimated.

"A'zi?" I say again. This time my voice reaches her, pulling back into the world.

As the father, Carlo is seated at the head of the table. A napkin is tucked into his undershirt. My aunt gets the second honor and is seated at the opposite end of the table, with me to her left. Like the fulcrum of a scale, Rosalba sits in the center, her role implied as she keeps the meal running smoothly, pouring water and wine and serving the food so that everyone ends up satisfied.

"More cheese, Papa?" Rosalba says, nervously offering a spoonful of grated cheese at her father. Carlo has more than enough cheese on his pasta already, and he waves her away.

The rest of us continue eating, but Rosalba's dish goes untouched. Instead, she sits on the edge of her chair, quietly nibbling on a piece of bread. She seems to be working up the courage to say something.

Suddenly, the courage comes and she flashes a big smile at my aunt. "Did Mamma tell you, Professoressa, that the wedding favors came in yesterday?"

My aunt nods mildly and continues eating.

Rosalba, disappointed that my aunt isn't interested in her news, goes back to nibbling her bread.

Delia, however, starts to laugh. It's a scornful kind of laugh, and I sense something is coming. Something that might cause more harm than good.

Rosalba frowns deeply. "What's so funny?" she asks her sister.

"Do you really think the Professoressa cares about your silly wedding favors, Rosalba?" Delia says.

Delia's mother glares at her youngest. Through clenched teeth, she warns, "Deliaaaa!"

Nunzia's warning stokes Delia's fire even more. "Really, Professoressa, what is your opinion? Is it better to have a stupid, ceramic bell on your shelf or a diploma?"

"Maaaamaaa," Rosalba whines again.

Nunzia turns to her husband. "Carlo, do something about your daughter!"

While Carlo occupies the seat of authority, it is Paolo who steps in. "Apologize to the Professoressa and your sister," he says to Delia.

"Me? You're the one who should apologize. Before the two of you met, Rosalba was on her way to being a lawyer."

"Rosalba never wanted to be a lawyer. Did you, *cara?*" Paolo asks Rosalba.

All eyes now turn to Rosalba. Even Carlo stops shoveling food in his mouth long enough to see how Rosalba will answer.

Rosalba looks down. Instead of eating it, Rosalba is now shredding the piece of bread in her hand. She doesn't say a word.

"Go ahead, Rosalba. Tell them." This time when Delia says her sister's name, I can hear the love in her voice.

For a minute, I think Rosalba might grab hold of the lifeline her sister is throwing her, but then my aunt pipes in. "Paolo takes his future seriously. It might do you good to be a little more serious, instead of wasting your time and everyone else's," my aunt says to Delia.

Paolo's expression turns righteous and smug. "Grazie, Professoressa. Thank you."

Everyone's attention goes back to their plate. Everyone, that is, except Delia. Her shoulders sag and the defiant spark in her eyes is snuffed out. At the end of the day, the only one who comes out the winner in all of this is Rocco, the family dog. When Marco plucks a meatball with his fork, it falls to the ground, where a waiting Rocco happily gobbles it up.

12.

After lunch is over, Delia gets up to help her mother and sister clear the table. As she reaches for my plate, I look at her, but she purposely avoids my gaze. That is when I know something has changed between the two of us.

For dessert, Rosalba and Nunzia bring out a large platter of figs and cheese, along with some homemade cookies Nunzia had baked that morning.

"Here, let me help," Delia tells her mother, as she begins clearing away some of the dirty dishes to make more room.

As Delia starts piling dishes up, I go to get up.

"No, Anna. You're a guest," Nunzia insists, as Delia disappears into the house.

As I bite into a cookie, the sound of water running and dishes and glasses clanking against each other tells me that Delia is washing the dishes. I tell myself that a little bit of space to collect herself is all that she needs. But when the water in the kitchen is turned off and the cookies and fruit are all eaten and Delia still doesn't return, that is when I start to worry.

No one else seems to care about Delia's absence. Marco and Carlo return to their card game, and Paolo goes back to his book, this time with Rosalba dozing against his shoulder.

I'm about to take it upon myself to go find Delia when my aunt suddenly says, "Anna, let's go."

"Already?" I say.

"Yes. The sun's given me a headache," she says, getting up to leave.

"Rosalba, go in the house and get the Professoressa an aspirin," Nunzia says.

Before Rosalba detaches herself from Paolo, or even before I can suggest that I go ask Delia for the aspirin, my aunt is already across the yard. "No, no. I have to go," she says.

My aunt grabs her purse and heads for the garden gate. With a quick goodbye and thank you for the both of us, I rush after her, before she completely unspools.

By the time we arrive home, my aunt is acting even more out of control than that day at the gas station. She mutters to herself as her nervous fingers attempt to undo the buttons on the cotton dress she'd worn to lunch. But when the buttons prove too difficult, she practically rips the dress off.

Most of my aunt's muttering is unintelligible, but she does express one sentiment quite clearly. "Those parents are wasting their money," she says.

My impulse is to defend Delia. I want to remind my aunt that some people would rather live their lives, rather than just read about life in some book. Given my aunt's state of mind though, making such an argument is useless.

Instead, I say, "Let me get you some aspirin."

When I bring her the pills, my aunt quickly downs them. It is another hour of her sitting in her chair, rocking back and forth, rubbing her head and groaning in pain.

Eventually, she falls asleep. I drift into my room and lay down, hugging my pillow tightly to my chest. Seeing her like this is frightening, so much so that when I hear the refrigerator door open later that night, I am relieved to hear the faint clinking sound of glass.

Other than the tired expression on her face, my aunt is her normal self the next morning. Even though my aunt is on an even keel, Delia is a no-show for the next three mornings in a row.

"Have either of you seen her?" I ask Giovanni and Arturo. Neither one of the boys has any news.

"Looks like she's staying back a year," Giovanni says, doing nothing to hide his satisfaction.

Arturo offers me a reassuring smile. "Delia will be fine. She's very smart."

While I appreciate Arturo's optimism, I can't help myself. Each morning, as the clock ticks forward and Delia is absent again, I get angrier and angrier. My aunt is to blame for treating Delia poorly, but it's Delia's fault too, for allowing her own hotheadedness to get in the way.

Without Delia, the only thing that is left to occupy my time is the translation for Marcovaldo.

"What do you have so far?" my aunt says, leaning over my shoulder to see what I have written down.

"I'm at the point in the story where a man named Amadigi discovers the mushrooms and Marcovaldo is afraid that this other man will eat the mushrooms before he does," I say.

"Excellent," my aunt says.

Arturo and Giovanni raise their eyes from their work and look surprised. Coming from my aunt, both of them know how rare a compliment like this is.

Because I am still angry with her, I purposely don't react. Right now, there is a very big part of me that doesn't want to give my aunt the satisfaction of knowing just how much her compliment does mean to me.

On the fourth day, after Giovanni has conjugated nearly all of his verbs into Latin and Arturo is reading from yet another book he's discovered on my aunt's bookshelf, Delia shows up. She is two hours late, but still, she is there. When she arrives, it is as if days of torrential rain have finally come to an end and the sun has appeared from behind the clouds, bathing everything in cheery sunlight.

When my aunt goes into the kitchen, the powder keg of feelings I've been sitting on for the past four days finally explodes. "Where have you been?" I say to Delia.

I must sound demanding, even possessive, because Delia's eyes widen in surprise.

"Do you really want to be left back in school another year?" I say to her.

"Uffá, Anna! You sound just like your aunt." Then, as if being compared to my aunt isn't bad enough, Delia dismisses me with the same hand-flipping gesture she usually reserves for her brother or anyone else who, in her mind, doesn't count.

But I want to count in Delia's life. Very much so. But with Giovanni and Arturo watching us, waiting to see what I will say next, there's nothing I can do or say in the moment to make Delia understand that I am not the enemy.

Finally, it is Arturo, not me, who manages to build a tiny bridge for Delia to walk over. "Here. It's all sharpened for you," he says, handing Delia a freshly sharpened pencil.

"Thank you, Arturo," Delia says, accepting the pencil. She opens her notebook to the page where she last left off.

Arturo glances at me sympathetically, which only makes the ache in me worse.

"Ah! Look who's decided to finally show up," my aunt says when she sees Delia.

Delia nods, but she doesn't look up to meet my aunt's condescending gaze.

Instead of leaving it there, my aunt chooses to turn the screw some more. "I told your mother that sooner or later you might get a little sense in that head of yours."

As if she is biting back her words, Delia clenches her jaw. Can I blame her? My aunt's persistent ridicule is both unfair and unnecessary. Like the butterfly Delia showed me when we were sitting near the fountain, Delia is trapped. What she needs is encouragement. And, while my aunt has given that encouragement to the rest of us, in Delia's case, she's given up.

Delia isn't the only one who feels trapped. I don't know how but, in that moment I decide that, together, we will break loose.

And any sympathy I have for my aunt? Well, that gets flushed down the toilet.

Butterfly Summer

A couple of days have gone by and the cloud that's been hovering over Delia seems to pass. She is back to being punctual, and she gets her work finished even before Arturo. The thing that doesn't go back to normal is the time the two of us get to spend together.

To the best of my knowledge, my aunt hasn't changed the rules. But Delia herself has changed. Once she's done with her lesson, she collects her things, forgetting all about me.

Today, as my aunt checks Delia's work, my heart sits heavily in my chest. All my attempts to pull Delia back toward me have failed. I've told her silly jokes, sided with her against Giovanni when he acts like an idiot, and I even gave her my favorite mixed tape because I knew she would love the songs as much as I do. But all I got in return for my tape was a polite thank you. Delia has frozen me out.

With three weeks until I leave, I'm beginning to give up hope. Even my heart is slowly limping back into the cold cave it inhabited before I came to Ischia and met Delia.

As my aunt stuffs Delia's paper into her accordion file, I have all but given up. Out of the blue, Delia looks at me and says, "Anna, are you coming?"

Delia's tone is so cool and indifferent, it makes my heart hurt. When she looks at me, it's as if I'm the family dog, that she's been given the annoying task to take out for a walk. The expression on Delia's face calls back into question that first day at the cemetery. I'm also reminded of how those women outside of the yarn store had whispered about Delia. Does Delia want me tagging along with her only because it helps her in some way?

Delia shifts her weight. I can tell she's losing patience and not willing to wait. My heart tells me it's better that I give up now to avoid further hurt.

Of all people, it is Arturo, who finally forces my hand. "What are you waiting for, Anna? Summer is almost over. There aren't a lot of beach days left." For someone as white and pasty as Arturo, it's an odd thing to say, but I listen.

On the corso, I am back to following a few paces behind. Before Delia turned cool, I'd imagined us as the two wings of a butterfly. We were separate but connected. And when we walked arm-in-arm, it felt as if we were floating above everyone and everything together.

Now, as I keep a bit of distance from her, I wonder if Delia and I had ever truly been in sync with each other or, perhaps, I'd just wished it true.

Delia suddenly stops, almost causing me to collide into her. "Anna, why are you so slow?" Delia says. Then, like a thread being pulled into a needle, she loops her arm through mine. "Come on. Move faster," she says.

With her arm wrapped around mine, I have no other choice than to keep up with her. Delia's body whether she is dancing or only walking moves differently than mine. While I lumber, Delia's hips flow sensually causing her left hip to bump into mine each time she takes a step. Although our bodies are covered by our clothes, this subtle contact unpacks what I'd managed to pack away these last few days.

"I have some gossip," Delia says excitedly, as we pass the fish store. Only the fish on their beds of ice can understand the shivery sensation shooting down my spine as Delia tightens her hold on my arm. Is this a signal that what happened last Sunday is behind us, and that I am more important than anything my aunt might have said?

Gossip doesn't matter. What does matter is that the tight bubble Delia has created around us doesn't pop.

93

Trying my best to equal Delia's excited tone, I say, "Tell me!"

"Marco says Roma met an older woman!"

"Really!" I say, continuing on with my fake enthusiasm. But if Delia cares, then so will I. This is how desperate I am to get back in her good graces. Because with each minute that goes by, I realize more and more that without Delia, I am a guppy yanked from the water gulping for air.

"And listen to this. She's married!"

Even though I could care less about the sleezy details of Roma's love life, this last tidbit does manage to shock me.

Now that she's shared her story, Delia drops her hand from my arm and we go back to walking in silence. It seems like just the right time to bring up what's been bothering me.

"Delia, the other day . . . at your house? What my aunt said about . . ."

Delia cuts me off. "How about a little fun?" she says, before I can say anything further.

Delia steers me in the direction of Bar Italia. As usual, an army of scooters is parked outside the café. Today, there aren't any boys.

"Everyone's inside watching the game," Delia explains, reading my mind.

Delia walks through the maze of scooters. Some of them are parked so close to each other that she has to squeeze herself past.

"What are you looking for?" I say, as she seems to be searching for one in particular.

"Here it is," Delia says, as she throws her leg over the seat. She rocks the scooter forward by its handles, releasing it from its kickstand.

"Delia!" I say. My eyes dart to the door of the café, expecting for the owner of the scooter to come rushing out.

"Relax," Delia reassures me. "It's Marco's. The idiot keeps the key to his bike in a little magnetic box stuck under his seat," she explains, as she feels under the seat. "Ah ha!" she says, when she finds the box with the key just where she knew she would.

Delia turns the key, and the engine coughs to life. "Hop on," she says.

Most people might not count borrowing your friend's brother's scooter as a crazy thing to do, but I've lived a pretty sheltered life. So this feels pretty crazy to me, as Delia wiggles forward on the seat, making room for me behind her.

Delia steers us into traffic. As we pick up speed, Delia's curls blow into my face. Is it the air or Delia who smells like warm jasmine?

"Hold onto my waist," she says, taking one of my hands and planting it firmly on her side. To balance myself out, I have to reach around with my other hand, encircling Delia in my arms. When we'd walked arm in arm, Delia had done all the touching. It feels odd but also strangely exhilarating to embrace her in this way. And when we hit a bump, I have no other choice than to hold on tighter.

I imagine other girls – my best friend, Alyce, for example – would not feel comfortable being so close to another girl. But Delia doesn't flinch as our bodies bend in unison as the scooter tilts along the curves in the road.

Maybe the attraction isn't just in my imagination?

Delia veers down a narrow street. Compared to the other more traveled streets that we've been driving on, this area is more private with large villas that sit behind high, stone walls.

The road dead-ends and Delia brings us to a slow stop.

"Where are we?" I ask.

"You'll see," she says.

Butterfly Summer

Beyond the dead end, I see dense forest. A well-worn path has been carved under the trees. As usual, Delia leads the way.

The trees create a welcoming coolness to the otherwise hot day, but when the path ends, Delia keeps going.

"Are you sure you'll know the way back?" I say, worriedly. With Delia, I've already jumped off jetties and stolen other people's scooters, what does the girl have up her sleeve next?

Picking up on my hesitation, Delias says, "Come on, Anna. Don't you trust me?"

For Delia, it's meant to be a rhetorical question. She's not about to slow her pace in order for me to give her my answer. But do I trust Delia? And what would happen if I, once and for all, threw all my insecurity out the window? What if I really took a chance and told Delia how I really feel? What if I stopped hiding my feelings and really lived?

The land suddenly pitches upward, and the trees begin to thin out until we arrive at a cliff overlooking the sparkling, emerald-green sea below us.

Delia closes her eyes and takes a deep breath in.

"It's amazing," I say.

"And the best part is it is just you and me. Not a lot of people know about this spot," she says.

Delia sits down on a flattened tuft of grass. I sit down next to her. She picks up a rock and tosses it off the cliff. She contemplates the rock for a moment. Did she make a wish? If she did, is it the same wish I am holding inside of my heart right this very moment?

Suddenly, she turns and looks at me. "Have you ever kissed someone?" she said.

My mouth goes dry and my stomach tenses as she looks at me, waiting for my response. "No," I say.

96

As Delia considers my answer, I can't help myself. I lean in and kiss her on the lips. Well, it's sort of on the lips. Due to the impulsive nature of my action, I haven't planned this out correctly and our mouths don't line up in the proper way. At least what I imagine the proper way to be.

Guided by impulse, but also because I have no clue what should come next, I lean back. Pathetically, I search Delia's face, waiting for her to react to what just happened. To my horror, Delia says and does nothing. Her expression is just blank.

"We should get going before Marco realizes what happened," she says, getting back up to her feet.

As she brushes the dirt off the back of her shorts, my ears buzz and the earth feels as if it's fallen off its axis. I feel as though I might throw up. By the time I finally do find the strength to pull myself back up on my feet, Delia is already a few yards ahead of me, acting like she can't get away from me fast enough.

When we arrive at the place where we left Marco's scooter. The taste of Delia's strawberry lip gloss still lingers on my mouth and the buzzy feeling inside of me continues. Delia gets on the scooter and starts the engine.

The last thing I want to do is get back on the scooter with its smallish seat meant only for one passenger. Not wanting to be left out in the cold for a second time, I get on, this time, careful to keep my hands to myself.

13.

The drive back to the café is a blur. The sparkling sea and lush flowers tumbling over stone walls are now just a meaningless jumble of shapes and colors. The scooter sputters beneath me and, when we come to a sudden stop and I slide forward, Delia stiffens.

How could I be so careless? Delia knows just how weird I am.

We coast into the piazza. The joyride Delia promised me has left me consumed with shame and joylessness and I brace myself for what might come next.

When we pull up to Bar Italia, a sizeable crowd has gathered outside in the street and someone in the crowd is yelling at the top of his lungs. "Assholes! Thieves!"

Delia steers us closer to the commotion. Along with the usual number of teenage boys, a few of the taxi drivers have also wandered over, curious what all the ruckus is about.

It is when I hear someone say, "Hey, Marco! Here's your thief!" and see the two uniformed police officers, that I realize Delia and I are in trouble.

The crowd parts. giving Marco a clear path to come rushing at us. "You think this is a joke?" He yells at Delia. Marco is so angry, his words are punctuated by the spit flying out of his mouth.

"Relax," Delia says, as the two of us get off the scooter.

With the mystery of the stolen scooter solved, the two police officers wander off, but the drama still holds plenty of interest for the rest of the crowd.

"Give it to her!" someone shouts. This boy is joined by a couple of others who hoot and clap, urging Marco to do something to show Delia that he's the boss, not her.

As the pressure to save face hangs heavily in the air, Marco shifts his weight. "You better pay me back for the gas you used!" he tells Delia, loud enough for everyone to hear it.

Delia crosses her arms over her chest, defiant. "Oh? And just where am I going to get the money?" Delia says to her brother.

Marco's face turns red, and he glances back at the crowd, who are waiting to see whether he truly is the wimp everyone believes him to be.

"I don't know, but you better find it," Marco tells Delia.

As I've seen her do so many times before, Delia flips her hand in the air.

Marco blinks nervously, but, to his credit, he doesn't let up. "Fine! Then I'll tell Papa," he says.

Although it's a tactic a small child would use, the threat works. The same shadow that had fallen over Delia's face that day at lunch, casts a gray pall over her face again.

Since I'm also partially to blame, I am about to tell Marco that I will pay him back the gas money when the man from the other day – the one with the patchy beard and the fancy, red convertible – comes driving up. "Hey! Move this crowd over so I can pass!"

The man is like Moses, parting the crowd as if it is the Red Sea. Instead of driving past, he stops in front of Marco, Delia and I. "What's going on?" he asks.

"My sister took my scooter. She used up all my gas," Marco sputters pathetically.

The man looks at Delia and, in that slimy way of his, he grins and says, "Is that true? Have you been a bad girl?"

If I had a bat, I'd hit the guy.

To my horror, Delia turns flirty. "Kind of," she says.

"I see." The man reaches in his pocket and hands Marco a few lira. "There! I've paid your sister's debt. Now, get out of the way so people can go by."

Marco takes the money and the man drives off. Marco quickly hops on his scooter and takes off.

With nothing left to see, the crowd disperses. All that is left is the mounting uneasiness between Delia and me.

This morning, as Giovanni stands up, reciting his conjugations aloud, my aunt taps her red pencil like a conductor keeping the beat of the orchestra. Three days have passed since the kiss, and Delia is back to being a ghost. This time, I'm afraid Delia might disappear for good. After the whole debacle with Marco's scooter, Delia avoided looking me in the eye. Clearly, she finds me disgusting and doesn't want to have anything more to do with me.

Giovanni continues his recitation. The house is ungodly hot today and a line of sweat collects on my aunt's upper lip which she doesn't even bother blotting away. Throughout this entire visit, I've tried hard not to see the obvious, but it's become impossible to ignore the truth. I *am* just like my aunt. It's not only the shapes of our bodies and the unruliness of our hair that is the same, but it's also the secret wars that rage inside both of us.

Giovanni finishes. He sits down in his seat as my aunt records his score in her gradebook.

Arturo says, "Bravo, Giovanni!"

Arturo has always been the kind one, while Giovanni acts stingily toward Arturo. Today, however, Giovanni smiles at Arturo and says, "Grazie, Arturo."

Arturo smiles a huge smile. Even though in another moment or two, Giovanni will go back to being mean to Arturo, I can't help but be jealous.

The doorbell buzzes. As my aunt goes to the kitchen to push the switch that automatically unlocks the door, my heart races. There's barely an hour left of lessons. Could it possibly be Delia?

My heart drops when Nennella appears at the top of the staircase. "Buongiorno," she says. She's holding a straw basket with a dishtowel thrown over the top. In that proprietary way Nennella has about her, she carries herself and her basket, toward the kitchen. "I'm going to go make myself a coffee," she says and off she goes.

"You can leave early today, ragazzi," my aunt says, picking herself up. She goes and joins Nennella in the kitchen.

Giovanni doesn't have to be told twice. He grabs his books and bolts down the stairs. To my surprise, Arturo stays back.

"I have something for you, Anna," he says. Arturo hands me a thin, white envelope. "It's from Delia. She told me to wait for everyone else to leave before giving it to you," he says.

Butterfly Summer

I take the envelope. Before I can form a question in my head, Arturo gives me - a shy smile and darts off, most likely hoping to catch up with Giovanni before the other boy gets too far ahead.

Inside the envelope is an unsigned note that reads:

There is a party tonight. I will come by to pick you up.
Tell your aunt we are going for ice cream.

I read the note over and over. Delia's words are less of an invitation and more of a mandate. The hard truth of it is that Delia expects me to be who she wants me to be and to do what I've always done, which is to follow her blindly. And just like she's always done before, Delia is using me to get what she wants, which is permission from her parents to be let out of the house – because I am the niece of the esteemed Professoressa. The good girl. At least that is the role I've always played in Delia's little charade. If only her parents knew the truth. That, I'm not good at all.

The only relief I have is that, at least for now, it seems as though Delia hasn't told anyone about me kissing her. If word does get around, the brutta figura my father warned me about will be mine, as well as my family's.

From the kitchen, the faint licorice smell of coffee, along with Nennella's loud, haughty laugh, awakens in me the hard truth. My aunt's reason, as well as my own, for never talking about the vials in the refrigerator is, like all the other uncomfortable secrets she and I carry; better to pretend they don't exist.

I read the note one last time. And just as Delia has done to my heart, I tear it into little pieces.

Nennella joins us for lunch.

"Tell me, Nennella. What else is new?" my aunt says, as she places a dish of food in front of me.

After the note, I have no appetite for food or gossip.

Nennella talks about one of her ex-students who had planned to be a doctor, but who is now employed as a pizzamaker in Naples instead.

My aunt, who remembers Nennella's ex-student, shakes her head. "He was so bright! What happened?"

"Oh, you know. People start in one direction and then all it takes is a little curve in the road, and they're following a whole new path. Not always a good one, either," Nennella says.

Without thinking, I interject. "Don't people get to choose what makes them happy?"

"Anna, what's wrong with you today?" my aunt asks.

"Nothing's wrong with me," I say, a bit too defensively.

My aunt regards me suspiciously. Have I given myself away?

"Eat before your food gets cold."

A wave of relief fills me.

I take a bite. The chicken has been cooked with onions, garlic, tomatoes and oregano, and where I didn't have an appetite before, I suddenly discover one.

As I continue eating, Nennella, leans in. "Speaking of students. What's this I heard about Delia stealing her brother's scooter?" Nennella asks my aunt.

"She didn't steal anything. She borrowed it from Marco. Then she returned it," I say.

Nennella smiles slyly. "I can see why you would think that way, Anna," she says.

I'm about to defend not just Delia, but myself when my aunt gives me a sharp look and says, "Anna, m*angia!*" Telling me to eat is my aunt's way of telling me to keep my opinions to myself.

For the rest of the meal, every bite tastes more and more bitter. I don't know who I am angrier with. With Delia for acting hot and then cold? With Nennella for all her badmouthing? Or with my aunt for cutting me off?

After Nennella leaves, my aunt says, "Anna, help me with the dishes."

Usually, she prefers to do the dishes herself. This is why, as I scrape off the last bits from the plates into the trash bin, I'm expecting my aunt to bring up the conversation at lunch.

Instead, my aunt says, "Did you like lunch?"

Figuring she just wants to keep it to safe topics, I go along with her and say, "It was probably the best chicken I've ever eaten."

"Chicken?" My aunt says. This time, it's not the heat, but the deep-in-her-belly laugh that she now laughs that causes her face to turn red.

"What's so funny?" I say.

When my aunt stops laughing long enough, she says, "That wasn't chicken. It was rabbit. Nennella's family raises them."

My memory flickers back to the basket Nennella carried into the house that morning. For some people it wouldn't matter. For them, a chicken and a rabbit are both food, one being no different than the other. To me, it does matter because, once again, someone else has decided for me, without taking my feelings into account.

Getting away from people who dictate what I should and should not want was the whole reason I'd come to Ischia. Yet, here I am again. When will I stop being everyone else's puppet?

As I scrape off the last dish, it is then that I decide. I will go to that party. Not for Delia, but for me.

There is one thing I fail to consider. These days, Delia isn't exactly my aunt's favorite person. Now that she's missed so many lessons, I doubt my aunt will allow me out with her.

Fortunately, or unfortunately, my aunt is stricken with a particularly bad headache tonight. As the variety show we always watch at night drones on, my aunt pinches the bridge of her nose. She gets up and goes into the kitchen. As the girl, whose beauty far exceeds her talent, croaks out the song, I hear the faint sound of tinkling glass coming from inside the kitchen.

By the time Delia shows up, my aunt is fast asleep.

"Wait till you see the house we're going to," Delia says, as the two of us walk together in the opposite direction of the piazza, toward the bus stop.

"How far is this house?" I say. Luckily, my aunt always keeps the key to the house on a little hook in the kitchen. That key, which is one of those heavy, old-fashioned types, is tucked in my back pocket. With the key, I'll be able to let myself in. Still, what if my aunt wakes up before that?

"Oh, not too far," Delia says in her usual breezy and assured way. On the surface, Delia acts as if nothing has changed between the two of us.

The bus stop takes up a piece of sidewalk near a malfunctioning lamppost. Other than the occasional light from the headlights of a passing car, Delia and I wait for the bus in the dark. If only the dark could erase that moment on the cliff, and we could go back to the way things were before.

If I'd just given Delia more time, maybe *this* would be the moment when Delia would have felt safe enough to kiss *me*.

As I struggle with all the what-ifs, the bus arrives.

The bus winds along the coast, until it takes a turn.

"How much longer?" I ask, as I press my forehead to the window, trying to gage the distance as we drive higher and higher up the mountain.

"A little more," Delia says, blithely. Apparently, the party is taking place at Davide Lupo's house, one of Delia's classmates.

"If I'm home late, my aunt will come looking for me in the piazza. Then she'll tell your parents," I say.

In some small way, my warning is meant to remind Delia that she's not above it all. But if I've given Delia any reason to be concerned, she shows no sign of it. In fact, it is not for another five stops that she finally pushes the large red button by the door, signaling to the driver that we want to get off.

Davide Lupo lives in a large villa tucked elegantly behind high, flowering hedges. As if she already knows her way, Delia bypasses the front of the house taking us to a stone pathway that runs along the side of the house. In the back of the house, we find an expansive patio arranged with tables and chairs and filled with people. There is a designated dance square in the center of the patio where people are dancing. And, above the patio, on a second-floor balcony, a DJ spins records on a turntable. Embedded in the turntable is a kind of multi-colored strobe light beaming down on the dancers below, turning the ordinary backyard into a club-like atmosphere.

As we make our way through the crowd, I notice that there are people who are a variety of ages. Most seem to be around Delia's and my age, but a few are closer to my parent's age, as well.

"Is Davide here? Should we go say hello?" I say to Delia, yelling over the music so she can hear me.

"Later," she yells back. "Let's dance," she says, pulling me onto the dance floor with her.

Just as she'd done that day at her house, Delia abandons herself to the music. This time, with all the people around me, I am careful. With the exception of a few times when I pretend I am copying her steps, I pretend not to notice her.

The DJ changes the record. "When Heart of Glass" comes on, Delia really goes wild. Soon, I find it impossible to keep up with her and I migrate to the edge of the dance floor.

After a few more songs, I lose sight of Delia altogether. No one seems interested in me, so I drift over to the refreshment table. For the rest of the night I eat my misery, while a young couple sit a few yards away from me, making out.

Did I really think Delia could ever see me in a different light?

As it's growing more and more obvious that Delia has indeed been using me, she shows up an hour and a half later. "We should get going," she says, the hair around her face is slightly damp from all the dancing she'd been doing.

The only thing I have to show for the night is an empty sleeve of cookies.

We walk toward the spot where the bus had dropped us off. A group of kids I recognize from the party are milling around.

Delia asks the kids how long they've been waiting.

"Too long," one of the boys from the group says.

Delia looks at her watch and bites her lower lip. Good! It serves her right to get in trouble! Then again, if Delia gets found out, so will I.

After another half hour with no bus in sight, some of the kids give up and go back to the party. Another group starts walking down the hill.

"Come on," Delia says to me, as we trail behind the group heading down the hill.

Remembering the distance both buses had climbed, I say, "If we walk all the way back, we won't get there till morning!"

"Who said we're going to walk all the way?" Delia says.

The windy road we take is dark. When we get to the next intersection, Delia turns to face a car that is coming from that direction. She proceeds to stick out her thumb.

"What are you doing?" I say, freaking out.

"What does it look like I'm doing? We're hitchhiking," Delia says.

Luckily, the car passes Delia up.

"If you think I'm getting into a car with a complete stranger, you're crazy," I say.

Even in the poor light, I see Delia making her all too familiar hand gesture to me.

The road is quiet, with not a lot of cars going by. When one does, Delia sticks her thumb up again, and I hold my breath. This one too ignores her.

In the not too far distance, the deep, growl of a motor echoes off the stucco houses. As the sound gets closer, Delia puts her thumb out again. To my horror, a familiar red convertible pulls up.

"*Buonasera,*" the man with the patchy beard says. "Can I give you a ride?"

Before I can tell her no, Delia jumps into the car and waves me over.

A quick survey of my surroundings reveals a small café. The sign on its door says *chiuso*. Closed. Since the first group of walkers is completely out of sight now, I have no other options.

The moment I shut the car door behind me, the hairy beast presses his foot on the accelerator. The car is a two-seater. Instead of squeezing in next to me, Delia has chosen to straddle the center console, a fact made more lurid given that Delia is wearing a short, denim skirt. Delia's hair whips with the wind as one of her legs dangles on my side of and her other leg touches the hip of the man driving the car.

"Are you having a good time?" the man yells up to Delia.

"Go faster!" she says, and he does. He steers us around the next bend and, when he shifts gears, his hand brushes Delia's thigh.

Instead of pulling away, as she'd done with me, Delia doesn't budge. She allows the man to continue fondling her with his big, hairy hand.

We are quickly approaching my aunt's house, and I am on the verge of vomiting when Delia tells the monster, "Drop Anna off here."

"Drop me off? What about you?" I tell Delia.

"Don't worry about your friend. I know where she lives," the man says with a smug smile.

If I was a better, smarter, stronger person I'd rip that grotesque smile off his face and drag Delia out of that car. Instead, I reluctantly get out.

The man shifts gears and drives off, while all I can do is watch the girl I love and who I'd so desperately hoped loved me, disappear into the night.

14.

The next day and the next day after that, Delia is once again a no-show. This time is different though. This time isn't about shame or hurt feelings. What concerns me is Delia's safety. Why didn't I pull her out of the car? Why had I just let her disappear into the night with that monster?

It all comes down to one thing. Delia is Delia. No amount of yanking or pleading could force Delia to do something she doesn't want to do. But why would Delia want to go off alone with that man?

My question is answered, in part, that afternoon as I'm helping my aunt clear the table. "After I'm done, I'm going to Delia's house to see why she hasn't been coming," I say.

"Don't bother," my aunt says, as she rakes the bread crumbs off the tablecloth with the side of her hand.

"Why? Maybe I can convince her to come back," I say.

"She's not coming back. Her mother called me the other day."

The fact that my aunt has been in communication with Nunzia comes as a surprise to me. It also makes me wonder what else they've been talking about and if these conversations ever include me.

Keeping my tone measured, I say, "What did she say?"

"That Delia got a job and she isn't returning to school."

"Is that even legal? Delia is only fifteen," I say.

As I watch my aunt push the crumbs toward the edge of the table, where her other hand can catch them, she says, "What can I do, Anna? It's what her parents want."

I'm not about to let this rest. I follow my aunt into the kitchen. "But you know how smart Delia is!"

"Nunzia said it's a good job."

"Where is this so-called job?" I say.

Usually, my aunt doesn't like when I act a bit too demanding, but today she yawns and doesn't fight. "I don't know what she's doing exactly, but Nunzia said that Delia is working at that big supermarket in Piazza Bagni."

A supermarket? Why would Delia give up her future to go work at some supermarket? It doesn't make sense to me.

Before I can ask my aunt anymore questions, she yawns again. "Will you finish up? I'm going to take a nap," she says.

My aunt leaves for her nap and I finish the dishes. It isn't until I put the leftovers in the refrigerator that I notice a whole new box of glass vials has replaced the previous empty one.

Butterfly Summer

Piazza Bagni is located midway up the side of the mountain. Unlike the piazza just off the corso, there is no pretty fountain at the center of this square, just a patch of weeds and a couple of benches in sore need of paint. Three- and four-story apartment complexes stand on the perimeter of the piazza, with the supermarket and a small barber shop being the only two stores.

As I sit on one of the benches, I study the people going in and out of the store, which doesn't even have a name, other than its obvious title of *Supermercato* painted in bright red letters on its window. Unlike the small mom and pop specialty stores that dot the corso, this supermarket is large and brightly lit and it lacks the charm of those other cute shops.

I step into the store and the illusion of spaciousness immediately shifts. The shelves are stocked, floor to ceiling, and the aisles are tight, making it hard for two people pushing carts in opposing directions, to pass each other. And it's hot.

For all the times Delia complained about my aunt's house, what lure does this cramped, airless place have for her?

I move past the aisles, searching for a familiar head of curly hair. It is back behind the meat case where I find Delia. She is dressed in a long, white coat with the markings of what I assume is the splattered blood of some poor dead animal.

I stay out of sight, hidden behind a display of pasta, as I watch Delia as she waits on a customer. "I'm sorry, *Signora*, but this is how you said you wanted your roast to be cut," Delia says, her tone uncustomary apologetic. A slimy blob of meat sits in Delia's ungloved hands and her curls are smashed down by a hair net.

The customer is an older, grumpy looking woman. "Keep your meat," she tells Delia. "You don't know what you're doing."

"Signora, please," Delia says, pleading with the woman.

"No, no," the woman says, as she starts walking away. "I'll come back when Signore Iacono is here."

When the woman is out of earshot, Delia whispers under her breath. "*Cagna.*"

When Delia finally sees me, her expression falls, but she quickly rebounds and smiles. "Anna!" She comes around the meat case, and gives me a big hug, making the moment even more awkward.

My plan is to stay calm as I try to convince Delia to go back to school, but something about that stupid hair net pushes my buttons. "What do you think you're doing working in a place like this?"

As she's done so many times before, Delia ignores my question. "Come, I'll show you around," she says.

As if I cared, Delia gives me a tour of the store, explaining how logically everything has been planned out.

When I can't take it anymore, I blurt out, "Why do you want to waste your life like this?"

Delia suddenly stops. She crosses her hands over her chest and glares at me. "It's a good job. Besides, what do you care? You'll be gone in a couple of weeks. And me? I'll still be here," Delia adds.

It's a point I've never considered, since I've only been focusing on what I was losing. Not the other way around.

Before I can argue my point and explain that I *do* care, a familiar voice yells, "Delia, where are you?"

The hairs on the back of my neck stand up. "That's not—"

Delia avoids my gaze and the confidence she'd exhibited while showing me around the store dissolves. Fretfully, she yells back, "Coming!"

As Delia turns to go, I shake my head. "Of all people? Why are you working for him?"

When Delia looks at me now, her expression is a mixture of indignance and anger. "Because not everyone is lucky enough to be the precious American niece of the Professoressa."

"Precious?" I scoff. "What are you talking about?"

"*Si!* You get everything handed to you on a silver platter. I bet you had to ask just once for a plane ticket and your parents bought it for you."

"Yes, but—"

"But what?" Delia says, not giving me a chance to explain that the ticket, like everything else in my life, came with strings attached.

The monster yells Delia's name again. The man is like an eclipse. Even when he's not visible, he blots out every bit of light and warmth.

Delia looks back over her shoulder, but she doesn't go immediately running. "Before I go, you have to promise me one thing," Delia says.

The idea that Delia still needs something from me fills me with a bit of hope. "What is it?" I say.

"Don't tell anyone about that night," she says.

Maybe because I've proven that I will always say yes to her, Delia doesn't bother waiting for a response. She simply walks away, her long white coat making a slight swishing sound.

15.

That night, I twist and turn. I can't get the smell of animal blood out of my nose.

The next day, I feel beat up. When Giovanni walks into the house, he is his usual self-centered self. But as Arturo settles into his chair, he shoots me a concerned look. While I've learned to like Arturo very much, I also know that the boy is like a microscope. And today, more than usual, I don't want anyone peering too closely, so I bury myself in my book.

For once, I am grateful for the distraction and, because my Italian has become quite good over these last two months, I am able to translate the last few pages of the story with ease. But when I come to the end, I can't believe it. After outwitting his enemy, Marcovaldo and his family finally have their mushroom feast, but the mushrooms are poisonous. In the last scene, the entire family ends up in the hospital needing their stomachs pumped.

Butterfly Summer

Two months of my life have been wasted on this story, just to be reminded that dreams are for pathetic losers like me and Marcovaldo!

I shut the book. "A'zi, the heat is making me sick. I need to go lay down."

My aunt surprises me when she says, "Today is too hot. Ragazzi, finish what you are doing and call it a day."

Once the boys are gone, my aunt surprises me for a second time. "It's too hot to cook. Let's go out for lunch," she says, reaching for her purse.

The fog that is my aunt's constant companion seems to have lifted temporarily. Unfortunately, it now hovers me. Listlessly, I follow her down the stairs.

As we cross the street, we pass the gas station.

"Ciao," Signore Chiachiaron says, waving to the both of us.

While my aunt is far from gushing, she, at least, waves back to her neighbor. It is the first time, I've seen her act with this much civility toward the man.

The restaurant my aunt chooses for lunch is located on the other side of the island.

"Aren't we taking the bus?" I say, as we pass the very bus stop where Delia and I stood waiting the night of the party.

"I can't take being wedged in like a sardine. No, we'll take a taxi," my aunt says, sounding more like herself.

The taxi we ride in isn't like one of those yellow cabs I've seen on the streets of New York City when my parents and I have gone to see the massive Christmas tree in Rockefeller Center. This taxi is an *Ape*, which in English means bee. With just three wheels, the driver sits up front, while my aunt and I sit in the back, a stream of fresh air blowing through the Ape's open windows.

116

My aunt shuts her eyes and takes a deep breath. Throughout my entire visit, I've never seen her this relaxed. On the one hand, I am happy. This is the aunt I'd hoped to spend my summer with. On the other hand, I can't help but blame my aunt for Delia's decision to throw her life away.

The restaurant is located in a pedestrian-only area, so the tax driver drops us a couple of blocks away.

As we walk toward the restaurant, we pass a number of shops.

"That would look good with your new hairstyle," my aunt says, pointing to a tortoiseshell barrette in the window of a small boutique. The shop is closed for the noonday meal. "On our way back, the store should be open, and I'll get it for you. Would you like that?"

My aunt looks at me expectantly. Like so many other aspects between us, my aunt and I share the same color eyes. Blue. But when my aunt is agitated, which is more often than not, her eyes turn gray. Today though they are a beautiful, clear blue, the same color as the sky.

Even if she refuses to stand up for Delia, the barrette feels like a peace offering of sorts and I meet her halfway. "Thank you," I say.

When we arrive at the restaurant, the owner greets my aunt with a warm hug. "Professoressa! It's been too long! How have you been?"

After my aunt introduces me, he shows us to our table. The table has a perfect view of the beautiful *Castello Aragonese*. The castle stands on a high perch of volcanic rock and its shape, carved out of craggy limestone, has always reminded me of the sandcastles I used to make as a kid.

"Forget about the menu, Professoressa. I am going to make you something truly special," he says.

After the man leaves, I say, "How do you know him?"

Butterfly Summer

"His daughter was one of my students. I helped her get into the University in Bologna," she says. Today, my aunt looks healthy and pink, without the permanent line of sweat marring her upper lip, and, when she speaks of her former student, my aunt lights up.

My aunt's pride for her student triggers me. "I don't understand, A'zi. If you can help this man's daughter, why won't you help Delia?"

My aunt frowns. "Haven't you heard the expression you can bring a horse to water?"

"Delia's not a horse," I say.

"No. She's a mule. And just as stubborn," my aunt says. "Now, please stop talking about this, Anna. I brought you here so we can have a nice day together."

Who is being the mule now?

Before I can argue further, the restaurant owner appears with a large bowl in his hand.

"Special for you, Professoressa. *Ricci di mare.*" He proudly places the bowl down in the center of our table. At the base of the bowl is seaweed, and nestled on the seaweed, sit a half-dozen round spiny stones. The stones have been split in half, revealing a center of yellow-orange goo that reminds me of egg yolks.

"*Fantastico!*" my aunt says.

"A man I know dives for them. They're only for my special customers," he says. "Enjoy!" Then he walks away.

My aunt squeezes a bit of lemon juice onto the goo, then spoons it into her mouth. She moans in pleasure. "Aren't you going to try one?"

I shake my head, revolted. It's not just the food that turns my stomach, but the way the man fawns all over my aunt. As she digs into another yellow yolk, a little bit of it sticks to her chin. I want to love her. And I do. But I also deeply resent her. I know it was Delia's decision to go work for that man, but if Delia felt the support not only from me, but from her family and my aunt, she might not have found herself in the hole she is digging for herself.

The man brings dish after dish of food. Other than a few bites here and there, I have no appetite.

My aunt looks at me. "Anna, why don't you just try?"

I can't resist the urge. "Oh, so now you want me to do something I don't want to do? Yet, you won't do the same?" I say, throwing my aunt's words back in her face.

A cloud of displeasure crosses her face and nothing else is said between us.

By the time we arrive at the dessert course, my aunt starts pinching the bridge of her nose. My aunt hastily pays the bill and we begin making our way back to where the taxi had dropped us off. On our way, the boutique is now open, but my aunt doesn't mention the pretty barrette and neither do I.

By the time we get back home, the fog that always seems to be chasing her, has caught up with my aunt.

Before we left for lunch, in a rare move, my aunt had left the windows open. But now, as if the bomb in her head might detonate at any moment, she commands, "Anna, quick! Close the shutters!"

I secure the latches, shutting out every last bit of light. When I enter the kitchen, my aunt is already holding one of the vials in her hands. She snaps the glass tip off, then pours the liquid into a glass. As she lifts the glass to her mouth and drinks, her hand shakes.

This time the medicine doesn't work the way it usually does, and my aunt now seems to be paying dearly for the few pain-free hours she'd enjoyed that morning. I follow my aunt to her room, helping her into bed. "*Gesú, Gesú. Aiutami tu,*" she moans to Jesus, asking him to help take away her pain.

Butterfly Summer

Even though the room is broiling hot, the pain is so intense that it causes my aunt to start shivering. I grab a blanket from the armoire and put it on her.

Despite her shivering, she kicks it off.

"A'zi?" I say, but her eyes remain closed.

My aunt's moans get louder. What should I do? Do I give her more of the yellow medicine? But what if it's too much?

With the time difference, my parents are asleep right now. And the idea of explaining this all to my father, whose limited patience might make matters worse, isn't appealing. I am about to look for Nennella's phone number in my aunt's phone directory when the sound of happy chit chat floats into the house from outside.

As I run out of the house, I'm not thinking clearly. All I know is that my aunt needs help *now*.

"Please! My aunt is really sick!" I say to Signore Chiachiaron.

The man is in the middle of fueling up a scooter, but he doesn't hesitate. He hands the nozzle off to the customer he was just helping, and sprints toward the house.

Signore Chiachiaron sits on the edge of my aunt's bed and gently taps on her hand. "Mareee . . . Mareee . . ." His voice is soothing, but persistent.

My aunt's eyes move under her closed lids, but she doesn't wake.

"Anna, bring me a washcloth and a bowl of cool water," Signore Chiachiaron says.

I am surprised that he knows my name, but I do exactly what he asks.

When I return, Signore Chiachiaron dabs the dampened cloth tenderly on my aunt's face. I refill the bowl whenever Signore Chiachiaron asks me to and, after about an hour of doing this, my aunt's moaning subsides and her eyes finally open.

"You're back!" Signore Chiachiaron says to my aunt, his voice sounding both tender and relieved.

As if she'd been traveling and suddenly returned, my aunt gazes up at her neighbor and says, "How long have I been gone?"

Signore Chiachiaron laughs and so do I, the relief I feel erasing all of the resentment I'd been holding inside of me.

Even though she is awake and the pain in her head seems to have subsided, Signore Chiachiaron continues holding my aunt's hand.

"How long have you been here?" my aunt ask him.

Signore Chiachiaron's answer comes in the form of a shrug.

"A while," I say. "He dropped everything when I told him you weren't feeling well."

"You better get back out there, Gaetano. Before you get robbed blind," my aunt says. This is the first time my aunt has called her neighbor by his first name.

A look passes between them. But before I can figure out what the look means, Signore Chiachiaron stands to go. "Anna, if your A'zi doesn't feel well again, make sure you come and get me. Ok?"

As I fluff my aunt's pillow for her, I say, "You really should go easier on him. He's a very nice man."

Whether it's the relief she feels or she is agreeing, all my aunt says is, "Mmmm."

16.

Slowly and over the next few days, my aunt regains her strength. Now that I'm done with Marcovaldo, she suggests another book.

Given how down I am about Delia, the last thing I need is another depressing story. "Can I help you grade tests instead?" I ask my aunt.

"Why not," she says.

That afternoon, she grades Giovanni's test as I grade Arturo's. Methodically, I work my way down Arturo's answers, comparing them with the correct ones on the master list. Like always, Arturo gets every answer right.

On the other hand, Giovanni's paper is less than perfect. As my aunt makes another red check, she wrinkles her nose. "Do you smell that?" she asks.

"I don't smell a thing," I say, quickly shooting down her suspicions. As kind as Signore Chiachiaron had been to my aunt, I know it's only a matter of time before my aunt's paranoia is reignited and things go back to the way they were before I got here.

Speaking of before I got here. In the last week, there's been a noticeable lessening of tourists coming in on the ferry. Pretty soon, it will only be a mere trickle and Ischia will be returned back to her grateful inhabitants.

Soon, it will be as if the summer never happened.

Almost.

My aunt puts down her pencil and rubs her eyes. "I can't believe the wedding is this Saturday."

"Wedding?" I say.

"Did you forget Rosalba and Paolo are getting married this Saturday?"

The wedding! With everything going on, I'd completely forgotten.

"We need to buy you a dress," my aunt says.

I hate dresses, but I'm not about to argue because this might be the last chance I get to see Delia before I leave Ischia. As well as my last chance to finally set things straight.

The moment we arrive at the church, a suit-clad young man rushes up to my aunt, extending his elbow out to her. As I follow the two of them down the aisle, I do a quick scan of the crowd. No Delia. I imagine she is tucked away, with the rest of the bridal party, in some backroom.

Then again, I wouldn't put it past Delia to not show up to her own sister's wedding.

The groomsman deposits us in the second pew on the bride's side.

"That is Paolo's side," my aunt says, gesturing toward the opposite side of the aisle.

Butterfly Summer

The guests on the groom's side all have the same pasty-white complexions and their scowls are identical.

The organist strikes a few keys and people turn to watch Nunzia, escorted by Marco, walk down the aisle. Marco looks awkward in his new blue suit. Whoever tied Marco's tie has pulled the knot too tight because he keeps tugging at his collar.

Before Nunzia takes her seat in the pew in front of us, she smiles proudly at my aunt. Meanwhile Marco and I regard each other like two animals unaccustomed to seeing each other outside of our usual habitat.

The rest of our pew is filled in by Roma and a man and a woman who, I can safely assume are Roma's parents, given their sharp jawlines and deep, dark tans.

Even though there are three people seated between us, Roma's cologne is so strong, it even overpowers the flowers. I sneeze. When I think back to that day when I first saw him and Delia's quick assumption, I have to laugh. If there's one thing Delia has taught me it's that love is more than skin deep. Love is a mystery that defies logic.

The organist begins playing with greater emotion. The only wedding I've been to was the daughter of a neighbor, but, from what I can tell, this wedding is playing out in the pretty typical way. Paolo enters from a side door, accompanied by a couple of stiff groomsmen.

The organist hits a note signaling for everyone to stand up. We all turn to face the back of the church. To my left, I can tell Nunzia is nervous. She is ringing her hands so hard, her skin matches the color of her pink dress. Is she that scared that the wedding won't happen? Shouldn't a mother be happy to see her daughter escape the same kind of servitude she's had to endure for so long?

Even if I could ask Nunzia these questions, I doubt she'd answer me honestly. Besides, what courage I have budgeted, I'm leaving for Delia.

Two bridesmaids walk down the aisle. From their indistinct features, I guess again that the girls are from Paolo's side. In fact, the more I look around, the more apparent it is that Paolo's side of the family dominates the ceremony. Their bland DNA is everywhere.

The next to come down the aisle is Delia. I am overwhelmed to see her. In contrast to the first two girls, Delia is like a ray of sunshine piercing through two dark clouds. Someone – I doubt Delia herself – has forced Delia's hair into submission. Her curls are piled high on her head, but a few stubborn tendrils have managed to escape. The ringlets gently skim her collar bone in a sexy way that makes my breath catch in my throat.

As Delia passes me, I silently will her to look my way. She doesn't and what courage I've collected shrinks a little.

Delia takes her place at the altar, and all eyes turn to Rosalba, flanked by her father. Poor Rosalba. As she walks down the aisle, her entrance is a bit of a snooze, compared to her sister's.

The ceremony drones on with Rosalba and Paolo standing and kneeling so many times I lose count. Delia performs her maid of honor duties perfectly. Each time Rosalba has to move – for instance, when the couple presents a bouquet of lilies to the statue of the Virgin Mary – Delia moves in tandem with her sister. To everyone else, Delia is the devoted sister. To me, she is a robot, playing out the part she knows she must play.

Once the priest announces the couple officially married, Nunzia's shoulders relax.

The reception takes place at a restaurant in a small hotel overlooking the sea. Compared to the number of people it needs to accommodate, the dining room is much too small. Making matters worse, Rosalba and Paolo have hired a six-person band, which makes it impossible to hear what a person is saying.

As soon as we find our table, my aunt yells over the music, "This place is too much. As soon as we eat, I want to go home."

This gives me almost no time to find Delia so that I can talk to her.

After Rosalba dances with her father and Paolo dances with his mother, the waiters come around with the appetizer. I notice Delia drift off from the rest of the bridal party.

"I need to use the bathroom," I tell my aunt.

"What about your melon and prosciutto?" my aunt says.

I say something about being allergic to melon and make my way over to the other side of the room.

But I'm too late. One of the groomsmen has already pulled her onto the dance floor. Like a dope, I stand there in my itchy, lavender dress, on the edge of it all, watching Delia dance. While, her feet and arms keep the rhythm of the music, in some ways, I don't recognize Delia. Just as she'd performed dutifully during the wedding, Delia's movements seem carefully measured, moving without that same appetite for life I've come to associate with her.

It's too hard to watch. I return to the table, and that is when I discover that my appetizer has been confiscated by the man seated to my right.

The wedding festivities continue and someone clinks their spoon against their glass. Her eyes closed, Rosalba leans toward her new husband, ready to kiss. All Paolo offers her in return is a quick, darting peck before he goes back to eating his lunch. As bland and joyless as the kiss was, I can't help but feel jealous.

Midway through the second course, my aunt says, "I'm ready to go."

"Already? But they haven't even cut the cake," I say, hoping for just a little more time. But what will more time give me? Not once has Delia looked my way. It's abundantly clear that she doesn't want to have anything to do with me.

It's a crushing realization.

"I would like something sweet," my aunt says, agreeing to wait for the newlyweds to cut the cake.

When my aunt becomes engrossed in a conversation with a woman at the next table, I decide to give it one last shot.

As Delia dances with yet another one of the groomsmen, Roma's cologne arrives, a few seconds before he comes to stand by me. "Are you having a good time?" he says.

Shrugging, I go back to watching the dancers. Well, one dancer.

Roma pushes his hands in his pockets in a bored kind of way. Whatever happened to the married woman with the villa, I wonder. Not that I care. The charade I played, in order to please Delia, seems laughable, now that I understand why being attracted to Roma is simply impossible for me.

Proving to me that he really is bored, Roma says, "Want to dance?"

Delia's dance partner keeps bobbing his head forward, an obvious attempt to get closer to her cleavage. This infuriates me.

Continuing his role as my decoy, I agree to dance with Roma.

Roma holds my right hand in his and places his other hand on the hollow of my lower back. Though we try our best, our two bodies don't seem to match up. I imagine it would be a completely different story if it were Delia and I who were the ones dancing.

Butterfly Summer

I step on Roma's foot for the third time, just as Delia and her partner come by.

"Ciao," I say.

Delia looks straight through me and says to her dance partner, "My feet hurt."

Delia walks off leaving her dance partner and I both disappointed.

Delia's indifference completely guts me. When I return to the table, my aunt wants to leave, and I am out of reasons to stall her.

Of all people to save me, it is Roma's mother who says, "We can drop you off at home, Maria. Let your niece stay a while longer. Don't you see, she's having fun?" Roma's mother winks at me.

Fun is the last thing I am having. Still, I am grateful for the extra time.

My aunt leaves with Roma's parents, as do many of the other guests. Without so many people around, I'm hopeful to finally catch up with Delia.

I find Marco outside on the terrace smoking. "Do you know where Delia is?" I ask him.

"She left," Marco says.

"Without bothering to say goodbye?"

My face must tell the story that's in my heart because Marco says, "Let her go, Anna. That one is trouble. Anyway, pretty soon you will be back in America, and you won't think of any of us ever again."

Marco exhales a long plume of smoke. Remembering what Delia said about Marco liking me, I set aside my own heartache for the moment. "That's not true."

Marco's eyes widen. I can tell by the way his Adam's apple bobs in his throat that he's swallowing hard and thinks I'm referring to him when I say this.

Well, at least one of us still has hope.

The seed of an idea begins to sprout in my mind. It's a seed that's been fertilized by heartache, hurt and anger. But I'll need Marco to bring my idea into full bloom.

"My aunt already left. Can you give me a ride home?" I say to Marco.

My reassurance to him that I would never forget this summer, coupled with my request, turns Marco red in the face. With total disregard for who might be standing on the terrace below us, he quickly tosses his half-finished cigarette over the terrace wall and says, "Let's go."

It's not until we exit the hotel, and I see Marco's scooter that the memories of that one astonishing afternoon with Delia come rushing back.

Am I sure I am doing the right thing? And is Delia the one I'm trying to help? Or is my own pettiness steering the ship?

Marco turns the key and the scooter wakes from its slumber.

This is my chance to change course. Instead, I yell into Marco's ear, "Before you drop me off at home, can you take me someplace first?"

Marco grips the handlebars tightly. "Oh?" he says, the hope and excitement in Marco's voice crystal clear, even over the noisy motor.

"Yes. Take me to Piazza Bagni," I say.

"Piazza Bagni?" Marco says.

Of all the romantic places Ischia has to offer, Piazza Bagni, with its sad little patch of grass, is an odd request. My idea has found firm footing and I am resolute. "Yes. Piazza Bagni."

Whatever my wishes are, Marco is eager to comply. He steers us onto the *corso* and turns off. As we start climbing up, like an old horse on its last leg, the scooter's motor moans.

Butterfly Summer

It is already past eleven o'clock when we pull into the square and many of the apartment dwellers have drawn their curtains for the night. Marco parks on the other side of the square, straight across from the supermarket. A neon sign I hadn't noticed before blinks brightly, on and off, like a fanged mouth opening and closing, threatening to eat us up.

Marco cuts the engine, and we both get off. My heart is pounding. I can safely assume that Marco's heart is also beating wildly, although for a different reason.

"Would you like to sit?" Marco says, pointing at one of the benches.

"If you don't mind, I'd rather walk," I say. What I'm about to do does not have to be done in any particular manner, but if I don't keep moving, I might lose my courage.

"Okay," Marco says, and we begin our stroll.

If anyone were to peek out from their apartment window in this moment, Marco, in his suit and me in my lavender, ruffled dress that my aunt insisted I buy, must look like any other young couple in the throes of a new courtship. While Marco is wishing this to be true, that impression couldn't be further from the truth.

The late summer air is like velvet. Somehow, this feels wrong to me, given what I'm about to do.

As we make it around the square, a fluttering sensation fills my chest. Is it wrong for me to decide what Delia's destiny should be? But, as we approach the supermarket, with its darkened windows and fanged, neon sign, the only thing I worry about is that it's not too late to pull her away from that monster.

"This is where Delia works, right?" I say, stopping and pointing at the store.

Marco, who's probably spent the last twenty minutes trying to work up the courage to hold my hand, frowns when I bring up Delia again.

"Yes," Marco says. "Are you sure you don't want to sit on a bench?" he says.

Ignoring the question, I say, "And you don't find it strange that Delia would want to work here?"

Marco sighs. "My sister has always done things her way," he says.

There's an edge in Marco's tone, and I can tell he's getting tired of the conversation. Before he gives up on me and insists on taking me home, I say, "There's a reason Delia got this job, Marco. It's not a very good reason."

Marco furrows his brows and looks serious. It's the first time he's ever looked at me in a way that has nothing to do with lust. "Is Delia doing something she shouldn't be?"

Up until this moment, I'd believed that, given his mild nature, Marco would use the details of that night of the party in the best, most diplomatic way. But his sudden and aggressive tone startles me.

"If Delia is doing something, you must tell me, Anna," Marco insists.

The flutter in my chest has turned into a hot, acid, which is now rising up into my throat. Glancing back at the darkened supermarket's darkened window, I see a beautiful girl with an ugly hair net on her head. This *is* the right thing to do.

When I am done telling Marco about that night, he looks as if he's in physical pain.

"Let's get you home," Marco says, as he quickly crosses the square. It's as if Marco can't get rid of me fast enough.

Back on the scooter, Marco pulls back hard on the gas. As we leave the square, I catch another glimpse of the neon sign. While I might have saved Delia from one monster, I fear I've just handed her over to another.

17.

O ver the next week, I worry about the seed I've planted in Marco's head. What happened that night, after Marco dropped me off? Did he rush home to tell his parents? Or did he confide it only in Delia, making her a deal that he would keep it a secret only if she promised to quit her job immediately? Each day, for the next week, I hold my breath, waiting for Delia to appear at my aunt's table, while these theories, and many others, run through my head.

On the last day of summer school, my aunt gives Giovanni and Arturo their certificates of completion. Over the last two months, Giovanni has sprouted up, his cheeks losing their childhood roundness. When he gets back to school, I am certain that all the girls will be chasing him.

Arturo, on the other hand, still presents himself as a shy, young boy, who still hangs on Giovanni's every word. Arturo is like one of the small volcanic rocks the litter the sand here in Ischia. If you look at the rocks up close, you will notice that some of them have a tiny mineral vein running through them. The tragedy of these rocks is that most people will never notice the depth hidden inside. They simply choose to walk over them.

Giovanni doesn't waste a single minute. As soon as he has his certificate in hand, he wishes me a quick goodbye and dashes away, chasing what little summer there is left to be had.

Arturo, on the other hand, dawdles for a few more minutes. He hangs his head and peers at me through his thick shock of bangs that hang like curtains over his brow.

"I hope to see you next summer," Arturo says.

Since that night in Piazza Bagni, the future feels as if it is pulling me forward. "I don't know. I'll be a senior this coming year. After that comes college," I say, making up reasons why it would be impossible for me to return. Besides my aunt, who is now talking about coming for a visit, what other reason is there for me to come back?

"Well, I hope you do," Arturo smiles.

As Arturo collects his things, I finally ask him the question that's been on my mind all these weeks. "Arturo, I'm curious. You're so smart. How did you end up in summer school?"

Arturo's only response to my question is a shy shrug. He gives me a quick hug before racing down the stairs, on his way to, no doubt, catch up with Giovanni.

The day before I am scheduled to leave, my aunt pulls my suitcase down from where it's been stowed away in the attic ever since I got here. I sit on a chair, watching her stuff packages of pasta, coffee, along with some of my mother's favorite chocolate and hazelnut *Bacis*. As usual, the shutters are closed, but the tile floor feels cool under my feet. The intense heat of summer is finally easing up.

I wish I could say the same thing about my feelings for Delia. Rather than dulling in intensity, the pain of what might have been feels like a thousand needles poking my heart.

Yesterday, I'd taken a walk on my own. Still unable to give up my hold on those beautiful days, I headed for the port. Once there, I climbed on top of the wall, walking the narrow parapet. Since falling in love was a lot harder, the idea of falling off no longer frightened me.

As I approached the rocks where Delia and I usually sat, a girl, with dark, curly hair, occupied one of the rocks nearby. The wind whipped the girl's hair, blocking her face.

Just one more time, God . . . just one more time.

But when the girl brushed her hair away from her face, it wasn't Delia.

"I hope this sweater fits your mother," my aunt says, pulling me away from my thoughts. Somehow, my aunt manages to stuff the sweater in.

"Nennella is going to complain," I say, with a laugh.

"Oh, who cares about that one," my aunt says and we both laugh together. Even though I still resent my aunt for not helping Delia more, the two of us have finally found our rhythm together. And now it's time to say goodbye.

I push away this sad fact and remind my aunt again. "You're coming for Christmas? Dad said he'll send you a ticket."

Instead of answering, she stands over my suitcase, examining it for more space. Just as it hasn't always been easy to understand my feelings for Delia, the same is true for my aunt. Our relationship is a lot like my suitcase – filled mainly with good things, but sometimes it becomes heavy, making it difficult to carry.

"Oh, I never asked what you thought of Marcovaldo," my aunt says.

134

"The truth? I didn't like it," I say.

"No? Why?"

"Marcovaldo just tries and tries, and, in the end, he's never able to get what he wants. So, what's the point?" I say.

"That *is* the point," my aunt says, but she doesn't elaborate. She just keeps looking at my suitcase, trying to figure out a way to fit more in.

On the day I leave, the air is thick with the threat of rain. Nennella is her usual blustery self when she arrives. "If it rains before we get on the ship, I swear!" she says with her fist in the air. Does Nennella honestly think so much of herself that she believes God will heed her warning?

Normally, Nennella's tantrums would annoy me, but, today I am grateful to have something else to focus on, other than Delia's empty chair and my aunt's sad expression.

Nennella takes my suitcase and starts down the stairs, leaving my aunt and I to say our goodbyes.

"Thank you, A'zi," I say. While there's still so much that's been left unsaid between us, I find nothing but love and comfort as I wrap my arms fully around my aunt's thick middle.

"Promise me, you'll write? But only in Italian!" my aunt says.

I laugh and give her another, long hug. If only my hug had the power to chase away all of her hard days.

A taxi waits outside. As the driver takes my suitcase from Nennella, Signore Chiachiaron yells over to me and waves "*Buon viaggio!*"

Still grateful for the way he'd come to my aunt's rescue, I wave back.

As the taxi brings us to the ferry, the first raindrops begin to fall and Nennella continues her bartering with God. "Hold off just a little longer!"

For my part, after no word from Delia, I've given up on God.

Our taxi pulls onto the dock and the exact thing Nennella has been praying against happens. The rain comes down in sheets.

By the time we take our seats on the ferry, the two of us are drenched to the bone. I peer out of the window next to me. As the glass is pelted with rain, the sun-drenched colors of Ischia are already beginning to fade.

The captain blows the horn, and we start to move away from the dock. Even though it's just gray and rain, I keep my gaze fixed, my heart holding on to the last tiny hold it has, before Ischia is completely out of sight.

Next to me, Nennella blots her arms and face with a bunch of napkins. "By the way, I saw your little friend this morning. She told me to wish you a good trip."

Shocked, I say, "My little friend? Do you mean Delia?"

"Yes. What other friends do you have?" Nennella says, snidely. "If you ask me, it's good you're leaving. That one's no good."

Fed up with Nennella's crusty attitude, I can't hold my tongue. "Don't talk like that. You don't know Delia."

Nennella crumples the napkins in her fist and stares at me. "And you do? Did you know she likes to get in cars with strange men? She's a real *puttana*, that one."

The word *puttana*, which means whore, is like a loud gong going off in my ear.

"Yes, someone told her brother, and her parents won't let her out of the house, except to sweep the sidewalk. That's when I happened to see her," Nennella explains.

The consequences of telling Marco the truth splash over me. Delia knows I didn't keep my promise to her, but does she understand my reason why? Do I? What part of my decision had to do with the fact that Delia didn't love me in the same way that I loved her?

Without regard for anyone else, Nennella tosses the damp napkins on the floor.

Searching for a clue to what Delia must think of me, I say, "Did Delia say anything else when you saw her?"

Nennella shrugs. "What more is there?" Nennella proceeds to pull a magazine from her purse, and she goes back to ignoring me.

For once, Nennella is right. What more is there?

TODAY

18.

As I make my way down the narrow ramp of the hydrofoil, the rain eases. The fine mist that replaces the rain casts a soft glow over the green hills. The impression leaves me with a sense of stepping back in time.

"*Prego*, Signora," a crewman says as he extends his hand out, offering to help me with my bag.

Forty years ago, I was a Signorina – a Miss – and now here I am a woman – A Signora. How has so much time passed? Yet the creeping insecurities of that time as a young woman still exist beneath my skin, which, unfortunately, is a whole lot flabbier.

"No, grazie. I can handle it," I tell the man. If nothing else, all the traveling I've done over the years for the show has taught me how to pack light. But, as I step onto the dock, it's not my suitcase that weighs a lot, so much as the events of that summer.

My phone pings.

Cheryl: *How's Ischia? As beautiful as the pictures?*

How on earth does Cheryl know my feet have just landed in Ischia this very minute? As I'm about to text her back, the driver of a delivery van advertising fresh buffalo mozzarella, nearly runs me down. Omitting my near-death experience, I text Cheryl back.

Anna: *Fine.*
Cheryl: *Fine? Just fine?*

As I weave through the chaos on the dock, three little dots jump on my phone. Without me around, she must be bored.

Cheryl: *Well?*
Anna*: I told you. As soon as the finale wraps and the house is sold, I'm out of here.*
Cheryl: *Really?*
Anna: *Really!*
Cheryl: *Just like that?*
Anna: *Yes! Just like that!!*
Cheryl: *If you say so.*
Anna: *Yes, I say so. lol*

I wait for Cheryl to text back. She doesn't. And this bothers me for some reason. Because I don't want to admit certain things to myself or have the time to consider right now, I pick up my pace.

Signore Pisani's office is located a couple of doors down from the pharmacy, on the other side of the piazza. As I head in that direction, I pass the fountain where Delia had pulled the water-soaked cocoon from the water. The basin is dry and dusty, littered with leaves and even a little bit of trash, but I can still recall the butterfly's wings, wrapped tightly around its body.

These day, gay or straight, it doesn't really matter. While a few people have come into my life over the years, rather than risk my heart getting broken again, I've preferred the safety of my own cocoon.

At his office, Signore Pisani greets me warmly. Though it is late in the afternoon, I'm sure, like most Italians, he's already had his daily quota of caffeine. Yet Signore Pisani insists on sending his secretary, Isabella, to get us coffee – from the same café Delia and I ate our ice creams all those years ago.

Before diving into the matter of my aunt's house, Signora Pisani begins with some friendly chitchat. "How was your trip? Did your husband join you?"

While Italy, like many other countries, has become more modern in their customs, I am not surprised that a man Signore Pisani's age would assume that a woman my age is married, and that my partner would be a man.

"Nope. No husband," I say.

Signore Pisani shakes his head in a manner meant to show sympathy. "I'm afraid Italy sees its fair share of divorces these days too. Too bad I don't practice family law because, I'd be sitting on a fortune right now." Signore Pisani winks and, even though his assumptions about life, especially my life, can't be further from the truth, I laugh at his joke.

"*Allora*, let's see what we have here," Signore Pisani says.

Once the finale was officially planned for Ischia, I promised myself that I would focus only on the business at hand. But, as soon as Signore Pisani starts combing through the mountain of papers on his desk, my curiosity gets the best of me.

"So, the buyer? Are they foreign?" I say.

Still engrossed in all those papers, Signore Pisani's guard comes down. "Oh, no. It is someone here from the island," he says. Realizing his slip, he quickly frowns and says, "Forget I said that." He returns to his papers.

"Of course, of course," I say, but this tidbit of information has only whetted my appetite even more.

Three deep furrows form across Signore Pisani's otherwise smooth brow.

"Is everything okay?" I say.

Signore Pisani takes his glasses off, leans back in his chair, and gives me a serious look. "I just remembered something. It concerns your television show," he says. "However, it will only be a small bother."

Before Signore Pisani can elaborate, his secretary enters the office. She is holding two small paper cups. When she hands me mine, the coffee is piping hot. I place it on Signore Pisani's desk, leaving it to cool down for a while. Signore Pisani, on the other hand, shoots his back as if it is a shot of Tequila.

"You were saying? About my show?" I say, starting to worry. Italy, after all, is famous for its legal loopholes, none of them, I assume, ever being just a *small bother*.

"The *Ingegnere Civile* has some minor concerns. That is all," he explains.

"Ingegnere Civile?" I ask.

Isabella, who has not yet stepped out of the office, quickly translates for me. "Civil engineer," she explains.

"What does a civil engineer have to do with the sale of my aunt's house?" I say.

Signore Pisani starts to explain, but when his English bogs him down, he points to Isabella and asks her to explain it all to me.

Isabella's English might be perfect, but what she explains to me is incomprehensible. "The engineer found serious structural defects in the foundation of the house," she says.

My coffee, which still rests on Signore Pisani's desk, is now cold and undrinkable. "Are you telling me that I've traveled all this way for nothing?"

"Not at all, Signora," he says.

"Signorina," I say, quickly correcting him.

"Signorina," Signore Pisani says, correcting himself. Though I can tell by the way he says it that he doesn't understand why, at my age, I would want to announce to the world that I am unattached.

"The deal is not dead," he says. "In fact, it is very much alive. The buyer still wants the house and plans to make all the necessary renovations to it once they are in possession. The problem is that the engineer believes that the foundation cannot support the weight of your cast and crew, not to mention the heavy equipment you will be bringing in."

The jet lag finally catches up with me and I lose my cool. "So, what the hell do I do now?"

"Simple. You find another location to film. At this time of year, when there are so few tourists in Ischia, you will have your pick of hotels. Your crew will be welcomed with open arms!"

I picture Avi sitting serenely on his favorite yoga mat. When I tell him we're going to have to add an extra million dollars to the already bloated budget, his chakras are going to explode like a Fourth of July fireworks display.

"And since Isabella grew up on the island, I've asked her to help you with finding the ideal location," Signore Pisani says.

I glance back at Isabella and now understand why she's been hovering this entire time. The girl is just a kid, no older than the age I was the last time I visited Ischia. And the only thing I was capable of doing at that age was putting myself into a mess, not digging myself out of one.

With no other options at my disposal, I say, "Fine."

Isabella claps her hands, heady with excitement. "I can't wait to work with you, Signorina," she says.

At least one of us is happy with this arrangement.

19.

Once I reluctantly agree to Isabella's help, Signore Pisani hands me a pen and says, "Allora! In order for us to confirm the sale, I need your signature on a few documents."

A few turns out to be enough pages to fill an entire library. I attempt to decipher the legal mumbo-jumbo, but weary, I give up and just sign away. For all I know, in addition to turning my aunt's house over, I am also selling my own home in Burbank, along with my shares of that new metaphysical app Cheryl convinced me to buy into.

When I am done signing my life away, Isabella, who might be young, but who also seems highly efficient, opens a drawer and hands me a familiar key. Sitting in the palm of my hand, it feels strangely warm, as if that night after Davide Lupo's party was just yesterday.

Signore Pisani tells me if I need anything, he is here to answer any of my questions. It's ironic since the one question I have asked him, he's refused to answer.

Isabella walks me to the door. "If you like, I can come with you. Me, personally? I don't like being in the house by myself," Isabella says.

Isabella is sweet. "I'll be fine. Thank you," I say. What Isabella doesn't know is that I won't be alone. The ghosts of my past will be in the house with me.

"Are you hungry, Signorina? At least let me order you a pizza. It will be delivered to the house by the time you get there."

"Thank you, but I'm okay," I say, wondering what else has changed over the last forty years.

I leave the law office. As I walk along the main corso, toward my aunt's house, it too has visibly changed. In a poor attempt to replicate the French Riviera, someone has decided to plant a line of towering palm trees all along the waterfront. While some people might like it or view it as progress, I don't. These changed details take away from my memories, which I realize are not all bad.

When I get to my aunt's house, I am startled by another, more significant change. Signore Chiachiaron's gas station is gone, completely leveled. The little hut where Signore Chiachiaron would go to get out of the sun has been removed, along with all the gas pumps. In its place, there is a tiny park with a patch of shade trees and a few benches. The revving engines and beeping horns, not to mention the lively discussions, have been replaced with bird song.

If my aunt was still alive, this change might have provided her with a sense of peace and calm. Then again, maybe not.

After having my own panic attacks, I understand what my aunt was experiencing. Ten years after leaving Ischia, that first wave of anxiety I experienced started as a tightness in my chest, mimicking what I thought was a heart attack. After a battery of tests, my doctor told me it was anxiety, not my heart. Next came months of trial-and-error finagling until we landed on just the right meds.

The meds work. When I remember to take them. This is why Cheryl is always on top of me.

While I didn't keep my promise to Delia, I had kept another promise. When I returned home that summer, I told my parents about my aunt's headaches, how she was always sweating, and her up and down mood swings. To their credit, my parents did their best. They asked my aunt about the glass vials in her refrigerator and my father asked my aunt for the name of her doctor so he could talk to him. But like many people struggling with mental illness, my aunt poo-pooed everyone's concern. Things went from bad to worse and my aunt never did come for Christmas that year.

Looking at what used to be Signore Chiachiaron's gas station, I wish for the sound of his lighthearted banter. I also wish someone had been able to pinpoint my aunt's mental health issues sooner.

As I insert the key into the door lock, I instinctively glance up at the balcony. A head of gray curls does not pop out from the window. What I do see is where the paint has peeled from the stucco and a few missing rail posts.

I step into the house and a chill runs down my spine. Four heavy-duty, metal latches now keep the cistern lid locked in place.

When I was a Junior in college, my mother called me to tell me what my aunt had done. The two of us cried for days, but my father remained stoic, trying to convince us and himself that it had all been a horrible accident. But my aunt's perfectly placed slippers, to the right of the cistern's lid was undisputable.

My father didn't allow me or my mother to come for the funeral. And when he returned home, there was a sadness in his eyes that didn't leave him until the day he died.

148

I step around my own guilt and grief. As I make my way up the staircase, my phone pings.

> Cheryl: *Does it feel strange to be back in the house?*

Is Cheryl having me followed? How does she know I'm in the house? That's right! The last time I traveled for work, I shared my location with her and never bothered turning it off. Not many Hollywood execs would share their location with their assistants, never mind their spouses, but I must admit, I appreciate Cheryl's small intrusion.

> Anna: *Guess what I'm looking at?*
> Cheryl: *What?*
> Anna: *The table where I spent an entire summer translating an Italo Calvino short story.*
> Cheryl: *Sounds positively scintillating.*

The space seems tighter than I remember. A shaft of light spills through the shutters, animating a cloud of tiny dust motes. There, in front of my eyes, appear the ghosts of my youth. Giovanni, with his deep brown eyes and cleft chin, acknowledges me with a jerk of his head. Sitting next to Giovanni, like a loyal pet, sits the ever sweet, ever sensitive Arturo.

Shortly after my aunt's passing, a letter arrived. The name on the return address was A. Buonparte. Because I'd never bothered learning his last name, it didn't ring a bell. Buonparte, it turned out was Arturo's last name, and his letter was filled with gratitude for everything my aunt had done for him.

"Had it not been for the Professoressa's kindness, along with her understanding of the workings of my heart, I would not be on my way to the life that is truly meant for me," Arturo had said in his letter.

Seven years later, after I'd already moved to L.A., my mother forwarded another letter to me. This time it was postmarked from Milan. Inside the envelope, I found a newspaper clipping from La Repubblica announcing that Dottore Arturo Buonparte had recently accepted a position in surgery at the Policlinico of Milan.

Because I'd sent Arturo my congratulations on his new job, another letter arrived directly to my address in L.A. less than a year later. This letter held an invitation.

Please join us in a celebration of love between

Arturo

And

Alberto

While Arturo's invitation had answered so many questions for me – namely, the real reason he'd landed in summer school that year – it had an unintended effect. It reopened an old wound. Why couldn't my aunt find it in her heart to help Delia, the way she had so obviously helped Arturo?

When I tilt my head to the side, there, in my mind's eye just the way I remember her is my aunt in her faded housedresses. She circles over the table, the crank of the potato ricer also turning. Why hadn't I appreciated her more? And what if I'd been better at expressing my concerns to my parents? Would things be different? The pain of not knowing, along with the guilt, is like shrapnel lodged under my skin.

Inspired by Arturo's letter, I decided to write to Delia, but the minute I dropped the letter in the mailbox, I regretted it. Instead of expressing my true feelings, I hid behind the details of my life, boasting arrogantly about my busy days of packed meetings and the after-dinner drinks I shared with B-rated celebrities at the Polo Lounge. Delia never wrote back. I didn't blame her. Still, this second rejection hurt worse than the first. It also cemented my avoidance to open my heart ever again.

As if she can sense the dark place I find myself, my phone rings. It's Cheryl.

"Hey, shouldn't you be asleep right now?" I tell her.

Cheryl laughs. "Asleep? It's nine in the morning here. I've been at the office for three hours already," Cheryl says.

I laugh, imagining Cheryl in her office, surrounded by every type of elephant paraphernalia and tchotchke imaginable. On those days when we work long hours, Cheryl might take a quick fifteen-minute nap on the chaise lounge that sits in the corner of her office. On the lounge, there is a needlepoint pillow designed in an elephant motif. Under her desk, there's a rug, also emblazoned with elephants. But, my personal favorite is Howard, the cuddly, stuffed elephant I named after a history professor who always put me to sleep. Whenever I need to decompress, I hang out in Cheryl's office and cuddle Howard for a little bit, while Cheryl and I shoot the shit.

"You feeling weird?" Cheryl says. Like her beloved elephants, Cheryl is intuitive.

"You know that movie where the woman goes back into her past?"

Of all the movies with similar storylines, Cheryl knows the exact one I'm talking about. "The one with Judi Dench where she questions whether any of it really happened?" she says.

"That's the one."

"And?"

"Well, it just makes me question a lot of things about life, you know?"

Cheryl cuts me off right there. "Anna, you're not Judi Dench! Stop being so dramatic and get on with it already!"

"Right. About that," I say. "There's a glitch."

I tell Cheryl about the civil engineer's findings and the added expenses.

"Don't worry about Avi. If you ask me, your bigger problem is Jacob." Chery says.

"Jacob? You think the rumor about a new job is true?"

"Maybe a new job. Or maybe not," Cheryl says, cryptically.

It's not just me who finds Cheryl easy to talk to, and it makes me wonder. "Has Jacob said something to you that he's sworn you to secrecy?"

"No. Let's just say I have a gut feeling."

Sensing that Cheryl doesn't want to talk about her gut feeling any more, I say, "What about you?"

While I mean to ask about her, Cheryl, who tends to be a very private person, thinks I'm referring to the office again.

"Katrina called," Cheryl says.

"Katrina? Katrina who?"

"The woman you had dinner with last month?" Cheryl reminds me.

"Oh, her," I say.

"Yes. Her. She said she's been calling your cell, but you haven't picked up. You wouldn't be ghosting her, would you?" Cheryl says.

"Me? Never," I say. "So, what did you say to her?"

"I took down the message, told her I would give it to you. I also asked her for her address."

"Her address? Why?"

"So I can send her one of those edible arrangements. It's the least you can do for the poor woman!"

I laugh, but this time Cheryl doesn't laugh back.

"I was hoping she would just give up after a while," I say.

"Oh, so you do remember her?" Cheryl asks.

"Yeah, I do," I admit, starting to feel guilty. "You know the only reason I went out with her in the first place is because my mother plays Mah Jong with her mother."

"Is that why you did it? To make your mother happy?" Cheryl says. "All I'm saying is this is the last edible arrangement I send out for you. Got it?"

"Got it." I think of Howard. I could sure use a cuddle right now. And some sleep. I yawn.

Cheryl gets the hint. "Go get some sleep, you heartbreaker you."

After I hang up, Cheryl's heartbreaker comment still stings. When it comes to other people's feelings, am I still the same careless person I was when I was a teenager?

When I walk into the bedroom, I discover that the bed is unmade. What did I expect? The Ritz? I search for a blanket in the armoire but find nothing. Wrapping my coat snug around me, I throw myself onto the mattress. Maybe it's the power of memories, but when I press my nose into the mattress top, I get a whiff of my aunt's freshly laundered sheets.

20.

Isabella arrives first thing in the morning. When she sees the shape the house is in, she says, "Signorina, wouldn't you be more comfortable at a hotel?"

While I would be more comfortable somewhere else, staying in my aunt's house not only feels like a duty, but also some sort of penance for what I failed to do.

"I won't be here for long so I'm fine. Really," I say.

"At least let me call my friend. She will put the house in order for you while we look for a new place to film your show."

Before I say no again, Isabella is already dialing her friend. I give in.

Once Isabella tells her friend about what I need, she says, "I've come up with some ideas for hotels." From the fashionable messenger bag she wears across her body, Isabella produces a print-out of five hotels located around the island.

"You've done a better job with this than some of the people that work for me," I say to Isabella as I review the paper. Under the name of each hotel, Isabella has noted the price for renting out each hotel for the time we will need it for filming, along with various details about the hotels themselves.

Isabella smiles big. "I am a big fan of *Bride-to-Be Italy*, so I understand the look you are after." Isabella says, sounding like a real pro. What Isabella is referring to is the Italian version of the *Bride-to-Be* franchise, which, like the other thirty-eight shows we have franchised around the globe, is quite popular.

"I've called ahead and explained to each hotel owner what you will need in terms of space and amenities."

Maybe it's the jet lag or the realization of just how quickly I need to turn this show over, but suddenly the floor beneath me feels as if it is tilting sideways, taking me with it.

"Are you okay, Signorina?" Isabella says, as I reach out to steady myself against the wall.

Because I've been through this many times before, I know the drill. I take a couple of deep breaths and quickly excuse myself. "I'll be right back," I say.

Isabella looks at me worriedly, and, as I head to the kitchen, she follows close behind.

The kitchen table with its two chairs is in the exact same spot where I last saw them. However, my aunt's pots, her dishes, and even the water glasses she used to drink down her yellow medicine have been cleared out by someone my father hired years ago to empty the house of most of her personal things.

From my pocket, I pull out the bottle of anti-anxiety meds. Even with Cheryl's reminders, I forgot to take them. Not having a glass, I use my hand to cup some water from the faucet and I swallow a pill.

"Would you like to sit down, Signorina?" Isabella says.

Isabella's sweet, empathetic nature only reminds me further of my own shortcomings and the heaviness in my chest increases. I nod. Isabella takes my old chair and I sit in my aunt's, as the two of us wait for the pills to hit my bloodstream.

After a little while, Isabella says. "My aunt suffers from panic attacks. So does my cousin. They both take medication for it."

"I appreciate you saying that," I say.

Isabella shrugs. "These days people speak more openly about these things. I think it's good, don't you, Signorina?"

"Yes. It is," I say.

We continue to sit there. After Isabella's initial comment about her aunt and cousin, she sits there calmly, waiting patiently as the heaviness in my chest begins to lift. When it does finally dissipate, I take a deep, fortifying breath.

Isabella's phone pings, and she reads the text.

"Whenever you are ready, the driver is waiting for us, Signorina," Isabella says, gently.

After another ten minutes, I feel like my old self again. "Let's do this," I say, reminding myself of the job I have ahead of me.

"I think you've missed your calling as a location scout," I tell Isabella as we take a tour around the first hotel on the list. The place is impressive and does suit the mood that our design team shoots for. "If you want, I can hook you up with a job in Hollywood."

I'm serious. Isabella has mad instincts for this type of thing and is able to point out the flaws and good points like a pro.

But unlike the millions of other girls who would jump at the chance, Isabella is flattered, but she is not interested. "Hollywood? Oh, no, Signorina. I would never leave my island."

"I understand completely," I say, knowing full well the strong tug Ischia can have on a person's heart.

There's something else I deeply admire about Isabella. At sixteen, she has a very strong sense of knowing where she belongs in the world. It's a trait I envy.

The first hotel Isabella has taken me to see is the Hotel Ischia Paradiso, a hotel which sits high upon a cliff, giving it a majestic view of the bay. The hotel manager, Signora Maio, a slender, elegant woman, shows us around the property. At the back of the hotel there is a stone staircase, covered with a rambling vine that, come springtime, will blanket the staircase in the color of ripe cherries. It is easy to picture Bianca, our show's latest bride-to-be, walking down those stone steps in her Vera Wang wedding dress. It is also easy to imagine Eric, the groom Bianca's chosen after televised weeks of deliberation, waiting for her on the sandy beach at the base of the cliff.

To go along with the beach-wedding motif, I jot a note down in my phone: Bianca, sandals, seashell motif.

Hmmm . . . Maybe we should eliminate footwear completely and let Bianca and Eric both go barefoot. Another wave of anxiety hits me, different than a panic attack. Are Eric's feet close-up ready? The guy played college ball, and football players aren't exactly known for their mani-pedi routines.

I dictate a text to Randy, one of my production assistants, who takes care of these types of loose threads.

Butterfly Summer

Anna: *Send me a picture of Eric's feet ASAP!*

Randy sends me an immediate thumbs up, without asking me why I would need such a thing. The two of us work in Hollywood where no request is ever too strange.

Signora Maio gives me an odd look. Without realizing it, the woman has been listening to me dictating into my phone.

"Your show is about feet, Signorina?" Signora Maio says.

"Oh, no, no," I say with a laugh. "Your hotel is beautiful," I say, quickly changing the subject.

I'm about to ask Signora Maio for a contract to sign, when Isabella pulls me aside and whispers so that Signora Maio cannot hear. "Don't make up your mind too soon," she says.

"Isabella, I'm kind of on a tight timeline here and need to make a decision fast," I remind her.

Isabella's lips turn downward. "Isn't the point of your show to find your heart's desire? And how do you know that you have the right one if you don't give yourself a chance to look around?" Isabella smiles at me. Her beautiful face brims with youth and optimism. Even though Jacob and the rest of the crew are set to arrive tomorrow, I can't bring myself to crush Isabella's spirit.

"Okay," I say to Isabella. "Let's see what else you've got."

Contrary to Isabella's expression, Signora Maio looks a bit sour when I tell her that I must think about it.

The driver Isabella has arranged to take us onto the next hotel is a young man named Luca. Luca opens the door for us as we exit Hotel Ischia Paradiso.

"I'm sure you will find the one, Signorina," Isabella says as we settle into the back seat and Luca starts the car.

"Yes, Isabella. I'm sure I will," I tell Isabella. What I don't tell the sweet girl is that something I've learned is that finding your heart's desire does not always mean you get to keep it.

The next two hotels are impressive in their own right. Hotel Smeralda has a large outdoor area with four pools and a dramatic waterfall, while La Grande Miramare boasts lush gardens and a pond dotted with giant lily pads. Just as Signora Maio had been, the other hotel managers are just as gracious and eager as they take me on a tour of their properties. And just as she'd done at the first hotel, Isabella continues pointing out the advantages our crew will have if we choose to film our show at each one.

Upon leaving La Grande Miramare, Isabella says, "Ready for the next one?"

While Isabella also has the stamina of a sixteen-year-old, at fifty-seven, my body is having a tough time shaking off the effects of jet lag. "I've seen enough," I say.

When I tell Isabella that she can go ahead and arrange things with Signora Maio, she claps her hands. "Ah! I knew it! It was love at first sight!" Isabella say.

"Yes, that's exactly what it was," I say, not wanting to burst Isabella's romantic bubble. But my choice is more practical than romantic since the ambient noise from the waterfall and pond at the other hotels could create a real headache for our sound team, while the stone staircase at the Hotel Ischia Paradiso would give our Director of Photography the money shot he is always after.

"How about some lunch? I think you've earned it!" Isabella suggests.

"Sure," I say. With just two cups of espresso in my stomach, I am literally working on fumes.

"I know of a good place that is not too far from here," Isabella says.

Because it is close, we end up walking to the restaurant. Along the way, Isabella points out plants, telling me their scientific names. "That is Nerium Oleander. And see this one? It is called Primula di Palinuro. In the summer it will have beautiful yellow flowers on it."

"How do you know all this?" I ask, fascinated.

Isabella shrugs. "When I like something . . . how do you say? I don't let go of it," she says. To emphasize her point, Isabella makes a grabbing gesture with her hands.

Isabella's laughter and her light step, remind me of how I'd felt around Delia. If I'd only waited a little longer and not scared her off like I had, perhaps life would have turned out differently. The problem with life, however, is that, once you choose a path, it's impossible to retrace your steps backward.

The restaurant is small and quaint. Other than a couple who sit in a corner conversing in German, it is just the two of us. The handsome, young waiter can't keep his eyes off of Isabella and keeps spilling the water every time he comes over to refill our glasses.

Once the waiter is out of earshot, I lean across the table and whisper to Isabella. "He's cute!"

With her eyes still on her menu, Isabella says, "I have no time for boys. Or for girls, for that matter."

Isabella's reaction catches me off guard. Along with her comments about her aunt and cousin, I am starting to see how more modern attitudes have begun to take root even here on this small island. Unfortunately, it's a change in attitude that is forty years too late for me.

I'm about to ask Isabella about her other interests when my phone starts to ping in quick succession. Avi has started a group text with Sam and Jacob piggybacking. The barrage of texts demand an answer for the same question. Have I found a location?

"Do you need to get that?" Isabella says.

"It can wait," I say, turning the sound down on my phone. The good food, wine and company I am currently enjoying is not something I want interrupted, especially by those three morons.

When my phone lights up with Cheryl's name, I say, "*Scusi*, Isabella. This is one call I do need to take."

On my way into the restaurant, I'd noticed a small alcove where an old phone still hangs on the wall. I head there and tuck myself into the small space.

"Ciao, bella!" I say, answering Cheryl's call on quite possibly the tenth ring.

"Whoa! Someone's had a few glasses of wine today." Cheryl laughs. "Is that why you've been ignoring all of Huey, Dewey and Louie's texts?"

"For your information, I haven't even finished my first glass. It's this place. It's getting under my skin, I guess. I kind of feel . . ."

"Like you're old self?" Cheryl says, finishing my sentence for me.

"Exactly!"

"Maybe you're just starting to remember who you used to be," Cheryl says.

"So, what's going on with Huey, Dewey, and Louie?" I say, quickly changing the topic.

Cheryl sighs, but she doesn't force the issue. "Having to fend off old girlfriends is one thing, Anna. But it's above my pay grade to deal with those three schmucks. So, deal with it!"

Butterfly Summer

Cheryl stops short of saying *or else*! Cheryl and I both know that working for me is no picnic in the park, and that she'd have plenty of job offers the minute she posted her resume. Because I don't know what I'd do without her, I quickly apologize.

"I promise. I'll answer them the minute I get off the phone with you," I tell her.

"Good!"

There's a pause on Cheryl's end.

"Is there something else you wanted to tell me?" I say.

"It's about that other thing. Have you decided?"

"No," I say.

"Well, you better decide before the whole circus comes. They'll be there tomorrow, and you might never get this chance again."

"I know. I know," I say. Until this moment, the smell of garlic that filled the restaurant hadn't bothered me, but I am starting to feel irritated.

"Where are you now?" Cheryl says.

"I'm about to have lunch. At a restaurant. Why?"

"Are you alone?" she says.

Cheryl's list of questions is starting to feel like an interrogation and this is completely out of character for her.

"No. I'm with my lawyer's secretary. She's the one who's been helping me to find a new venue for the finale," I say, my voice more snappish than I intend it to be.

"I see."

"Cheryl, what's going on with you?"

From six-thousand miles away, Cheryl manages to jump down my throat. "What's wrong with me? You're in Italy and I'm over here cleaning up all your crap!"

"Oh," I say. "Well, if it makes you feel any less jealous, the sixteen-year-old girl I'm having lunch with is nowhere as capable at putting away a bottle of Chianti the way you are."

Cheryl snort-laughs hard in only the way Cheryl can. And much in the way I miss cuddling Howard, I realize that I also miss Cheryl's snort.

After promising Cheryl I'd bring her back chocolate, pasta and, of course, wine, we hang up.

I return to the table. In my absence, a breadbasket has been placed in the center of the table.

"Everything good?" Isabella says, as she nibbles around the edge of a piece of bread. She eats like a little mouse and reminds me of someone else who used to nibble at her bread.

I lie. "Yep. All good," I say. Even though Cheryl and I had ended on a good note, the conversation between us has left me a bit confused.

Before I can sort things out in my brain, the waiter comes back. He takes Isabella's order first. When it is time for him to take my order, his gaze remains on Isabella, and he doesn't even bother writing my order down.

Once he goes to give the order to the chef, Isabella leans forward, her expression changing from sweet to somewhat sneaky and clandestine. At first, I think she is about to agree with me about the waiter being cute, but she surprises me. "I heard from Signore Pisani that you're curious about the identity of the buyer?" Isabella says,

Normally, it's not my style to discuss such things with a sixteen-year-old, but Isabella has already proven that she is not typical for her age. "I am curious, but whoever the buyer is, they're working pretty hard at keeping their identity a secret," I say.

"If you want, I can find out more information for you," Isabella says. It is not just her youthful spirit that reminds me so much of Delia, but also the conspiratorial tone she uses, that draws me back to that time in my life.

"Won't it get you in trouble?" I say, not wanting to cause Isabella any drama to her own life. "What about your job?"

Isabella shrugs. "Trouble makes life more interesting, Signorina. Besides, Signora Pisani is my uncle, my mother's brother. My mother will kill him if he fires me!" Isabella picks up another piece of bread and starts nibbling. "Besides, it will be fun!" Isabella says.

"May I ask for another favor?" I say.

"Whatever you like, Signorina," Isabella says.

I reach into my purse and pull out a pen. On a paper napkin, I write down Delia's name. "Maybe this is a long shot, but could you try to find this person for me?"

On the napkin, I've also written down the name of the street where Delia and her family lived forty years ago.

"I'm not sure if she still lives at this address," I say, thinking about how many times I, myself, have moved over the years. Then again, Isabella's sense of permanence might not be a rarity on an island where families live in homes passed on from one generation to the next.

Isabella reaches her hand for the napkin, but I hold back.

"There's one other thing. If you do find this woman, I don't want her to know that I am here."

"I understand," Isabella says, without blinking. In this way, Isabella reminds me less of Delia and more like a mini-Cheryl, cool and efficient, but also capable of seeing right through to my deepest motives. But, unlike Cheryl, Isabella is much too polite to tell me what she really thinks of me.

I slip the napkin across the table and Isabella deposits it into her purse without looking. She waves the waiter over, telling him that we would like more bread.

21.

After lunch, Isabella calls Signore Maio, confirming that we do want to use her hotel for the filming of our finale.

"Was she happy to hear the news?" I ask Isabella once she is off the phone.

Isabella shrugs. "Happy? Yes. Surprised? Not really."

"No?"

"Signore Maio could tell the minute you saw her hotel that you wanted it for your show," Isabella says. "You're one of those people who wears your heart on your sleeve, Signorina."

"That's not what Cheryl says."

"Who is Cheryl?" Isabella says.

"My assistant. According to her, I keep my emotions under lock and key."

Isabella tilts her head and looks at me quizzically. At first, I think it's because she's never heard the expression *under lock and key* before, but then she says, "Who knows, Signorina. Maybe you needed to come to Ischia to find the key to unlock whatever this Cheryl person thinks you are holding back from."

"Are you sure you're just sixteen?" I ask Isabella.

"At least that's what my birth certificate says," Isabella says with a laugh.

Luca stops the car in front of my aunt's house. Before I get out of the car, I point at the spot where Signore Chiachiaron's gas station used to be. "Do you know the man that had the gas station that used to be in this spot?"

Isabella shakes her head. "For as long as I can remember, it's been a park."

"What about him," I say, gesturing toward Luca.

"Luca is new to the island," Isabella says.

As I get out of the car, Isabella waves. "*A domani.* I hope you have a more comfortable rest tonight, Signorina!"

When I enter my aunt's house, it's as if an army of elves has been hard at work all afternoon. The house is dust free and I can breathe without sneezing. The tile floors are freshly mopped, and the bed has been made up with fresh linens. In the bathroom, there is a set of matching bath towels, along with soaps and other toiletries. In the kitchen, I find cups, dishes, forks, and spoons, even a bottle of water, a bottle of wine, a nice slab of provolone and a box of crackers for a midnight snack. The best thing I find is a bag of freshly ground espresso and an espresso pot, very much like the one my aunt used.

I open the bag and smell. Now that I am an adult, coffee and heaven are one in the same. All these items make the house feel more like a home again, though one thing is still missing – my aunt. What I'd give to sit again at the kitchen table with her, finally telling her all the things that have been locked up in my heart for all these years.

I kick off my shoes and pour myself some wine. Glass in hand, I wander back into the living room. The elves have left one of the shutters open. Instead of looking at my phone, I take a chair and listen to the sounds floating up from the street – cars and scooters zipping by, mingled with bits of conversation, and music playing on a car radio as it passes. I sip my wine and breathe it all in. I've communicated all the details to the other key players, and I've asked Isabella to find out about the buyers and Delia. The rest, as Dante Alghieri, the famous Italian poet, once said is in the hands of destiny.

My phone rings. This time, the minute I pick it up, I confess my guilt to Cheryl right away. "You caught me! I just finished my second glass of wine and was considering a third," I say, with a laugh.

"You're going to need that third one on account of what I have to tell you," Cheryl says.

"What's wrong?"

"Your precious bride-to-be Bianca? She wants out."

"What are you talking about? Out of what?"

"The show, Anna. She doesn't want to get married to Eric."

"But *she* chose *him* out of a pool of thirty other guys. Why the sudden change?"

"Get this," Cheryl says. "She says he chews with his mouth open. She doesn't think she can handle a lifetime of living with an open-mouth chewer."

"Did our legal team explain that, unless she wants to bankrupt not only herself, but her children, grandchildren and great-grandchildren, that it's too late for her to pull out of the show?"

"Yes. It was also explained to her that, once the show is over, she's not under any obligation to stay married to the guy. She can simply file for an annulment. So, no harm, no foul."

"Please tell me she went for it."

"Nope. The girl is a cockeyed romantic. She says that, when she does get married, she only wants to do it once because then it will be forever."

"I can't friggin' believe this," I say, pouring myself that third glass of wine.

"Brace yourself," Cheryl says.

"There's more?"

"Yep. Her lawyer found a loophole in the contract."

"Our contracts are ironclad!"

"Apparently not. Because we changed the location, it creates a material change to the contract—"

This time it's my turn to finish Cheryl's sentence. "And a material change makes the contract null and void," I say.

"Exactly!"

There it is again! Italy messing with me again! Anyone who wants to do anything in Italy needs to have their head examined!

"What do the three Stooges have to say about all of this?"

"Avi and Sam are doing damage control as we speak."

"What about Jacob?" As the rest of us are stuck on a sinking ship, I imagine Jacob sitting with his feet perched on his desk, laughing at us.

"Funny enough, Jacob has been the only levelheaded one around here. He convinced Bianca that she needs to show her face in order not to get sued by the network. Jacob personally escorted Bianca onto the plane," Cheryl says.

"This is a disaster," I say.

"Not necessarily. The way you've talked about Ischia all these years, the place sounds pretty darned magical. Maybe some of Ischia's magic will rub off on Bianca, and she'll fall back in love with Eric. And the viewers will get the happily-ever-after ending they expect from us."

"You sound just like Isabella."

"Isabella? Who's that?"

There it is again, the same strange tone Cheryl had when she asked me about who I was having lunch with that afternoon.

"Isabella is the sixteen-year-old niece of my lawyer. She's the one who helped me find the hotel for our shoot," I say, purposely omitting the other things I've asked Isabella to help me with.

"Well, if you can't have me there to help you, Isabella sounds like a perfectly reasonable replacement," Cheryl says.

"Replacement? Didn't they break the mold when they made you?" I laugh.

Cheryl does not find my joke funny. "Yes, well, I should get going." Cheryl hangs up without so much as a goodbye.

The bottle of wine is nearly empty. I pour the rest of it in my glass, adding to the regret I already feel.

The entire cast and crew descend upon the Hotel Ischia Paradiso the next day and Signora Maio is quickly rethinking her choice. "All these lights, the wires and plugs! You're going to blow my hotel up!" Signora Maio says, fretfully.

The hotel's lobby is littered with at least a hundred large Pelican boxes, each of these boxes holding the cables, lights, cameras and the rest of the equipment needed for the filming of a large production like ours.

As Signora Maio nips at my heels like a nervous Pomeranian, I assure the poor woman. "Signora, my crew is very professional. They've worked under the most extraordinary conditions. I assure you that no one will plug a single electrical cord in before they know for sure that your circuit box can handle it."

The truth is that the only real way to know if the hotel can handle the wattage is to cross our fingers and hope it works. But, at least for now, Signora Maio accepts my story.

"Now, if you will excuse me, Signora," I say. "I must go to work."

My work in this moment is a cigarette. Coffee isn't the only thing I've acquired a taste for over the years. From time to time, when my stress level shoots through the roof and I need a little something extra beside my meds, a cigarette and a little Jack Daniels are just the things to keep me from jumping off the ledge.

Reminiscent of the last time I smoked here, I find a private spot, behind a row of tall bushes and away from all the chaos, where I can light up in peace. Fortunately, or unfortunately for me, my skills as a smoker have become more sophisticated over the years. Inhaling deeply, the nicotine begins the work of calming me down. At least for a few seconds.

When I first arrived at the hotel that morning, I found a message waiting for me. It was from Jacob. He explained that he was dealing with the whole Bianca situation in his own way and I should in his words *Stay Away!*

What the hell is he up to? While I didn't appreciate the tone of Jacob's message and have no idea what he means by "his way," there are plenty of other things for me to focus on. Like the paper Isabella handed me when she and Luca showed up at my aunt's house to drive me back to the hotel.

"What exactly am I looking at?" I asked Isabella, in between bites of the fresh *cornetti* she had also brought me.

Isabella explained. "The first name written down is the name of the estate that is buying your aunt's home."

"Whose estate?" I asked.

"That isn't clear," Isabella said. "Whoever the person is, they've worked very hard to keep their identity a secret. I did find some other papers that indicate that, once the transaction for the property is completed, the property will be registered with the state."

"The state? As in the government? Why would someone do that? It's just a house, not Fort Knox or the Vatican."

"I am not clear on this detail either, but, I agree, it is unusual."

"What's this other name?" I asked Isabella. "Hotel Gatopardo? But we already have the hotel for our filming."

Even though Luca was the only one within earshot, Isabella spoke quietly. "The Hotel Gatopardo refers to your second inquiry," she said. "The first address you gave me was sold a few years back and a new family is living there. But I asked a few people if they recognized your friend's name, and one of my cousins said that the owner of the Hotel Gatopardo has the same last name as your friend. Of course, I asked him to not say anything," Isabella said.

"Of course," I said.

Now that I'm in the thick of things, there's no time to think about any of what Isabella has told me. I carefully snuff out my cigarette and throw it into a nearby ashtray.

When I emerge out of my hiding place, I find David, my director, along with the assistant director, the director of photography and all the other department heads discussing where to set up the cameras.

"We need everything in places by one, so we can run through rehearsals and be ready to shoot by no later than three," David tells the group.

As with the rest of life, timing is everything. David's goals is to roll camera at that perfect time of day that everyone in the biz refers to as the golden hour. The golden hour creates a warm, glow, giving life – or in our case love – the illusion of perfection.

I send Jacob a quick text.

Anna: *Rehearsal for one! Doable?*
Jacob: *Totally!!!*

For Jacob, who would stab someone in the eye with a pencil if that person took the last piece of sushi from Jacob's plate, his text, with the accompaniment of all those exclamation points, strikes me as strange. Maybe it's not a new job, but a new prescription that's led to Jacob's change in personality. Whatever it is, I am relieved that Bianca is back onboard.

I go back to discussing lighting options and the way the dramatic close-ups should be framed when my phone pings.

Isabella: *I'm sorry to say that this piece of news is sad. The man who owned the gas station died many years ago.*

The news of Signore Chiachiaron's passing does not surprise me, but it does feel as if yet another brick from the past is being kicked away from my foundation.

When Signora Maio had given me the tour, she'd pointed out the hotel's bar located on the outside patio near the pool. Normally, I'm not much of a day drinker, but, as a gesture to Signore Chiachiaron, I decide to honor the man with a private toast. It's also a way to get away from all the other craziness.

When I take a seat at the bar, the barman says, "What can I get you?"

I scan the bottles behind him, my eyes settling on one in particular. "I'll take a glass of that," I say.

The barman pours the liquor into a fluted glass and hands it to me. "We are famous for our limoncello. Did you know that?" he says.

"I did know that," I say. After that, he leaves me alone.

Instead of drinking the bright, yellow liquor, I lift the glass up to the light. Regardless of the way my aunt had treated him, Signore Chiachiaron never judged my aunt. And neither do I. But instead of drinking the liquor, a thought occurs to me and I rest the glass on top of the bar and text Isabella.

>Anna: *Do you have time to take me to the Hotel Gatopardo?*

Isabella's response is immediate.

>Isabella: *Sí*

From my pocket, I pull out some money and set the euros down on the bar, the still filled glass catching the sunlight.

22.

Before I go to meet Isabella, I decide to check on Jacob's progress with Bianca and to let him know I'm stepping away for a couple of hours, but that I'll be back.

Knocking on the door to the bridal suite, Bianca grunts out "Come in!" The tone of her voice is less than cheerful and, when I enter the suite, I discover a very different scenario than the one Jacob led me to believe. There, in the most expensive room in the hotel, lying flat with her arms flung out, is Bianca. A satin sleep mask covers her eyes and, as I approach her, I can hear her whimpering, like a tiny puppy left on the side of the road.

"What's going on, sweetheart?" I say, trying my best to remain calm.

In response to my question, Bianca raises her right arm and makes a thumbs-down gesture.

"Sorry to hear that, sweetie," I say, as I fight the urge to dump a bucket of cold water over her head. Since signing her, Bianca has been the most difficult and demanding bride-to-be we've ever had in the history of our show. And given the number of years we've been on air, along with all our foreign spin-offs, this is saying a lot. The girl is a brat with a capital B!

The suite isn't just one room. It is a series of rooms. It's so big, in fact, that it could double as a whole apartment. In addition to suitcases filled with makeup and clothes, the room is littered with half-drunk cups of what looks and smells like some kind of herbal tea and an empty vodka bottle.

"Where's Jacob?" I say.

My question triggers another chorus of groans from Bianca.

Far from being my favorite person, I can't blame Jacob for abandoning his post. Bianca is the ultimate Zen killer. I bet if I went looking for him, I'd find Jacob on one of the hotel's patios, decked out in his favorite spandex onesie, doing yoga, trying to shake off all of Bianca's bad juu-juu.

Knowing Isabella will soon be here, I take matters into my own hands. I plop myself on the edge of Bianca's unmade bed and pat the rumpled comforter next to me. "Come. Sit next to me, honey," I say.

Like a petulant two-year-old, Bianca sighs. She flips off her sleeping mask and does what I ask. While she might be a headcase, Bianca is also quite stunning. Her long black hair requires just a quick raking of her fingers to look picture perfect. The same goes for her makeup. Just like every other young girl on Instagram, Bianca spends a mint to have the latest, buzzy blush or newest fake lashes, but she need not bother with any of it. She's gorgeous without a lick of any of that stuff. Even her lips are pouty and full, with a natural cherry sheen that doesn't require lipstick. And, when she hasn't been consuming a case of Vodka, her complexion is bright and dewy. If it wouldn't create a riff with the union, I could've redlined the makeup and hair team from the budget completely.

But as with many things in Hollywood and in life, looks can be deceiving. The other side of Bianca's story – the part that is only hinted at judiciously in the editing room – is that the girl is just another frightened twenty-five-year-old with major abandonment issues. It's this vulnerability that turned Bianca into last season's fan favorite of the *Bride-to-Be* sibling show, *Groom-to-Be*. Bianca's soft side and her vulnerability spoke to the hearts of millions – that, and the vicious way she slipped a laxative into her rival's tea. Poor Missy. Talk about every action having its consequences. While the consequences Missy suffered were gross, it also made for some pretty funny TV. The fans loved it. So much so that the show's social pages were blowing up, demanding Bianca be chosen for top billing for the next season of *Bride-to-Be*.

While Bianca's antics make for good drama, they also drive me crazy. And since Jacob has defected to God knows where, it's up to me to get the ship back on course.

"Tell me, honey. What's going on in your heart?" I say to Bianca.

"I can't do it. I just can't," she says.

"Can't do what?" I say. I stroke Bianca's hair, trying to soothe her, when what I really want to do is pull her hair out by its roots.

Bianca is terrible at using her words, and she just goes back to groaning and sighing.

My phone vibrates in my pocket, most likely Isabella letting me know she's here and is downstairs waiting for me. To make it to the Hotel Gatopardo and still stick to the filming schedule, I need to make my point with Bianca quickly.

"Honey, is this really about Eric's chewing? You know, no one is perfect. The point of any relationship is to learn to navigate through those difficult times and grow together." My advice is far from fresh. It's plagiarized from Oprah. Or maybe it was Dr. Phil. Ironically, it's not even necessarily anything I personally believe. But if it's good enough for Oprah and Dr. Phil, then it should be good enough for Bianca.

"It's not just chewing. It's about that too," Bianca says, pointing to the garment bag with the Vera Wang logo stamped on it. Vera Wang and Prixie have worked together from the beginning. We love Vera, and she loves our brides. She also benefits handsomely from all the attention our show gives her.

"I'm confused. Vera makes all our dresses custom. Girls die to wear a Vera on their wedding day!"

"No, the dress is perfect," Bianca says.

The carbs from the pastry I ate that morning have burned through my bloodstream, and I am beginning to crash. With as much patience as I can muster, I say as sweetly as I possibly can, "Then what *is* the problem?"

Bianca's perfectly toned shoulders slump. She waves her hand around the upgraded room and says, "Up until this point, love has just been helicopter rides, candlelit dinners, pretty dresses, and fooling around in the jacuzzi. But that's not really love, right?" Bianca asks me.

Bianca's sudden existential crisis feels like a well-earned slap in the face. Years ago, when I was working as a low-level production assistant for a then small company named Prixie Productions, I'd conjured up the idea of a dating reality show. As Bianca has just reminded me, I was utterly naïve about love, my vision horribly distorted by what had transpired between me and Delia. The best I could come up with was some crazy, fantasy version of what true love should look like. For some reason, my vision resonated with millions of other people.

Still needing to work myself out of this pickle, I push my own disappointments about love aside and reach for some other expert advice.

This time I quote Buddha. Or maybe it's Wayne Dyer? "Bianca, love is just perception. What you think about it is what you end up creating," I say.

Bianca stares at me, but her expression is flat.

I give her a pat and, as if I'm speaking to a small child, I say, "I need to run off to another meeting now, but don't worry. The next time I see you, you'll be wearing that gorgeous wedding dress, right?" I say.

Bianca doesn't say a word, and I have no time to wait around for any promises. As the door shuts behind me, Bianca lets out another whimper.

As the elevator descends to the ground floor, I text Jacob.

> Anna: *WTF!!! You said you had this figured out!*

The little dancing dots on my cell phone indicate Jacob is texting me, but then the dots disappear. What the hell is up with him?

According to Cheryl, the Prixie team is starting to lawyer up. While my hardened Hollywood heart takes comfort in this, I can't help but feel guilty. Sure, I gave up on love long ago, but what kind of ogre am I to push a girl into a loveless marriage, even if the marriage only lasts long enough for us to get it on tape?

I exit the elevator into the lobby again. The space is even more jammed packed. A huge ride-on-dolly that looks kind of like a ride-on lawn mower and is used for push-in and push-out shots by the Director of Photography, sits in the middle of the lobby. A special crane will lower the ride-on dolly down the cliff, positioning it on the beach in order to get that money shot David is banking on. The rest of the crew, which is made up mainly of twenty and thirty-something year olds, are uncurling extension cords, unpacking camera lenses, and generally making final adjustments, until the moment our assistant director, Sarah, announces that it's time to roll camera.

As I cross the lobby on my way to the main entrance, Signora Maio is noticeably absent. The poor woman has most likely given up and has taken refuge somewhere, probably counting down the minutes to when we are gone, and she can reclaim the peace and calm of her hotel.

Before I reach the door, I hear David call out, "Anna! I need you!" David makes a beeline straight for me, his harried expression indicates this can't be good.

With so much to juggle already, I can't imagine adding one more thing to my plate.

"I'll be right back!" I yell back at David. With that, I bolt for the door.

As I catch my breath, Luca drives Isabella and me toward the Hotel Gatopardo.

"Are you okay, Signorina?" Isabella says.

I glance at Luca. Isabella reads my mind. "Luca, do you mind raising the partition?"

Luca presses the button that raises the privacy partition turning the back seat into a makeshift confessional booth and Isabella the oddest of priests.

"Tell me, Signorina. What is on your mind?" Isabella asks.

Because Isabella is close to the age I was when I met Delia, I figure she might understand. Leaving the details about my aunt out, I tell Isabella all about that one special summer and how I ruined it all.

When I am done, Isabella looks at me with absolutely no hint of judgement in her face.

"Please don't be so hard on yourself, Signorina. You were just trying to protect the person you loved," Isabella says.

"You make it sound so easy, Isabella. But I don't think it is that easy at all."

"Signorina, haven't you heard that humans always make life more difficult than it has to be?"

I laugh, but it's not because I disagree with Isabella. Rather, it's the opposite. For someone so young, the girl has her shit together better than all the adults I know.

"If you want to find her, Signorina, I will do everything in my power to help you," Isabella says.

The combination of not being judged for my actions, along with the prospect of finding Delia and making things right, fills me with a huge sense of hope. That is until the car comes to a stop and Luca taps his fingers on the partition, his signal that we've arrived. The hope inside me is now replaced with abject fear.

The Hotel Gatopardo is what the average Yelp reviewer would call no-frills. A series of cracked steps leads us into the lobby, which is a bland space made up of patchy, white walls. A few planters, with limp, brown plants, are someone's poor attempt at sprucing up the place. A hobbled-over man in a threadbare, blue blazer stands unceremoniously at the reception desk. As we approach, he quickly stubs out his cigarette and waves the cigarette smoke away.

In the car, Isabella came up with an idea, and she takes the lead.

"Do you know my cousin, Franco? He works here," she says to the man, as I stand a few steps behind her, half expecting that my past will jump out from behind one of the wilting plants.

"I do know Franco," the man says. "You just missed him, in fact."

Isabella and I are both keenly aware of the fact that someone named Franco works at this particular establishment, given the fact that, as we peered through the car window, the two of us saw a uniformed employee whose name tag read Franco, exit the hotel.

Isabella continues the ruse. "Are you sure he's gone?" Isabella says with a pretty pout "He promised to meet us."

"Perhaps, I can help you," the man says.

"Perhaps. You see, the Signorina has come all the way from New York."

The man looks at me oddly. Who can blame him, given the fact that I'm wearing the dark sunglasses Isabella insists I wear in order to conceal my identity.

Butterfly Summer

"The Signorina is a big shot," Isabella says, really laying it on thick. "She needs a place to hold a meeting for her very wealthy business clients. I, of course, immediately thought of the Hotel Gatopardo."

I can tell by the way the man is rubbing his stubbly chin that he's having a hard time believing that, of all the swanky hotels in Ischia, anyone's first choice would be the Hotel Gatopardo.

"I can't leave my post because, as you can see, I am quite busy," the man says.

Aside from Isabella and I, the lobby is completely empty.

"Is there someone else that can show us around? Maybe the owner of the hotel?" Isabella says.

A lump forms in my throat at the mention of the hotel's owner.

"Let me see if she is available," the man says.

A plug-in phone hangs on the wall behind the desk, another sign of how behind the times the Hotel Gatopardo is. The man picks up the phone receiver and pushes a single button. In the not too far distance, there is a low buzzing sound. The man mutters to the person on the other end and hangs the receiver back on the wall. A minute later, the sound of clicking heels against tile floors gets louder and louder as a person comes toward us. All this makes my heart beat wildly in my chest.

The minute I see her, my mouth turns dry as the desert. Forty years has completely transformed her. In contrast to her surroundings, she is dressed sophisticatedly, in a linen skirt, blazer and high heels. Her hair, though now flecked with gray streaks, is pulled back into a sleek ponytail. The change that is most apparent and remarkable is her demeanor. There are no traces of the once nervous bride. In front of me stands a mature and elegant woman.

182

When she smiles, it is only with polite regard, an indication she does not recognize me as the niece of her former professor.

"Buongiorno," Rosalba says. "I understand you are looking for a hotel to hold a conference?"

Isabella glances at me. With a subtle shake of my head, I let her know that this woman is not Delia, but that we should still proceed.

I let Isabella do all the talking, explaining to Rosalba the reason for our visit. Even if it wasn't part of our plan, I am afraid that if Rosalba hears my voice, she will put two and two together.

"Let me show you around," Rosalba says cordially.

As ramshackle as it appears, the hotel is quite large. Rosalba brings us to a meeting room and, as she talks about the arrangement of tables and the room's capacity, Isabella says, "The man at the desk mentioned this is a family run hotel?"

"Yes. The hotel was originally owned by my in-laws," Rosalba explains. "After they passed away, my husband took it over, but now me and one of my siblings run it."

Forgetting that I'm there only to listen, I say, "You work with your sibling. That's nice."

Rosalba regards me, and I hold my breath. What if Rosalba recognizes me and tells Delia? Will Delia just run away from me again?

But Rosalba shows no signs of knowing who I am. Instead, she says, "Yes, family became very important to me, especially once my divorce was finalized. Let's just say my lawyer was a much better negotiator than his lawyer," Rosalba says with a smirk. "Come, let me show you the dining room where the attendees of your conference can have their meals if they choose."

The dining room is as bland and uninspired as everything else that we've seen. "This room can accommodate a hundred and fifty people, but if we open up those sliding doors, we might be able to squeeze in another fifteen," Rosalba says. "And if you are in need of any other services, such as transport to and from the airport and to the ferry, I am well connected to many reliable people. Just say the word, and I will be happy to help."

While her hotel is no-frills, Rosalba carries herself with confidence and poise. Seeing how this once domesticated, little mouse has now transformed herself into a keen businesswoman gives me hope that Delia has also become an independent, happy woman.

Isabella continues to probe. "What about staff? Do you have enough to handle such a crowd?"

"We have some staff, but mainly it's me and my brother Marco. He's around here somewhere if you would like to meet him," Rosalba says.

Taking a chance with Rosalba is one thing, but Marco will certainly recognize me the moment he sees me.

Isabella reads my face. "That's quite all right. I think we've seen all that we've needed to see. Thank you so much for your time, Signora," she says to Rosalba.

"Signorina," Rosalba quickly corrects her.

As Isabella quickly steers me away, Rosalba calls out to us and waves, "Let me know your decision!"

As we quickly make our way through the lobby, the man in the blue blazer is smoking again, our quick escape enveloped in a haze of cigarette smoke.

23.

The minute we get back in the car, my phone rings. It's David again.

Before I can even say hello, David starts yelling through the phone. "Anna, where are you?"

"I'm on my way. I'll be there in time for the golden hour," I assure him.

"Fuck the golden hour! We have bigger problems! Bianca is gone!" David says.

This time it's my turn to yell into the phone. "Gone? What do you mean gone?"

Isabella looks at me, startled.

"Makeup went up to her room, and she's nowhere to be found!"

"Sit tight. I'll be there in ten minutes." Before I hang up, I add, "And, David, *do not* mention this to anyone!"

I hang up and pinch the bridge of my nose as a huge headache starts to build up at the base of my skull.

"Luca, can you pick up the speed?" Isabella says. She rummages through her purse, pulling out a bottle of aspirin. She hands me a pill and a bottle of cold water.

"You're a godsend, Isabella," I say swallowing the aspirin.

"Signorina, now that you know that there is a connection between your friend and the Hotel Gatopardo, would you like me to do more digging?" Isabella says.

Being this close to finding Delia does the opposite of what I thought it would do. It causes me to freeze in my tracks. Just because Rosalba and Mario seem to be doing well in their lives, this doesn't guarantee the same is true for Delia. "If you don't mind, Isabella, if you could just concentrate on that other matter."

"Of course, Signorina," Isabella says, but I detect a hint of disappointment in her voice.

Disappointing people is one of my superpowers, unfortunately.

Luca pulls into the hotel driveway. My headache is beginning to subside just in time for me to deal with the next one.

Even though I've asked him to keep this all on the down-low, the minute I walk into the lobby, David rushes at me in a frenzy. Right behind him, looking a lot more relaxed than David, is Jacob.

Pointing at both of them, I say, "Both of you, follow me. Now!"

On the day Signora Maio gave me the tour of her hotel, I took note of the private office located just behind the main reception area. This is where I lead both bobos now.

Signora Maio is sitting at her desk when we enter. "Scusi, Signora Maio. Do you mind if we hold a private meeting here? It's an emergency. Otherwise, I would never ask."

Signora Maio arches her brow at us but relents. Once she closes the door behind her, I get straight into it.

"What the hell! I leave for an hour and the whole production turns to crap?" I say.

David repeats what he's already told me about Bianca being M.I.A.

"Did you search the property?" I say.

"I told a few people I could trust not to say anything to go look for her. Nothing," he says.

To Jacob, who is standing in the corner and being uncharacteristically quiet, I say, "You were supposed to be keeping an eye on her!"

Jacob shrugs. "I told you she was a loose cannon," he says.

At the end of last season, it had been Jacob's choice versus my choice for who would be the next bride-to-be. Jacob had opted for Sandy, a pert, little blonde, who had about as much personality as a packing peanut. My choice, of course, had been the fan's choice – Bianca. In the end, Jacob was voted down by Avi and Sam. This, and possibly the fact that Jacob has another job waiting for him, are just two of the reasons he would love to see me fail.

A thought pops in my head. I go to the door and there stands Signora Maio, pretending to work, when it's obvious that she's just been eavesdropping this entire time.

"Signora Maio, can you check to see if Bianca Longobardi's passport is still in your safe?"

"Certainly," she says.

In Italy, hotels are obligated to register every guest's passport and some, like the Hotel Ischia Paradiso, holds their guests' passports in a safe, returning it to the guest when they check out.

As we wait for Signora Maio to check, Jacob bites his lower lip. He's probably hoping Bianca is long gone just so I will make a fool of myself in front of Sam and Avi.

Butterfly Summer

Signora Maio returns. "I checked with our concierge. He said the Signorina's passport is still in our possession, safe and sound, and she has not officially checked out."

Letting out a sigh of relief, I thank the Signora for her help.

"At least we know she is still in the country. And, with the little time she's been gone, she's most likely still in Ischia," I say to Jacob and David.

Jacob is quick to steal my win, however. "We're still without a bride, Anna. Just give it up already. Bianca told you she doesn't want to marry that guy. Maybe we can get a couple of the writers to work something up real fast, something quirky and fun. Maybe a spontaneous dance contest on the beach! You'd be up for that right, David?" he says.

At nineteen, David had been the youngest director to ever win an Oscar for best short film. The only reason we have him is because, aside from his golden statue, David also has two ex-wives he is currently court-ordered to pay alimony to every month.

Alimony aside, David still has his standards. "I don't do quirky," David says, his voice flat. Clearly, Jacob has insulted David's artistic aesthetic.

Whether I'm trying to convince them or myself, I downplay the problem. "This is all textbook pre-wedding jitters. All we have to do is find Bianca and talk her down off the ledge!"

"Since when are you an expert on love, Anna?" Jacob says, hitting below the belt.

Jacob's comment stings more than he could possibly know, but I push back speaking the Hollywood language of money. "Listen, guys. Right now, we have network shareholders waiting for us to deliver them a huge profit margin. If we don't deliver, I hope you'll like your new job working drive-thru at In-N-Out Burger."

"If money is all you care about, Anna, then I'm out of here," Jacob says, storming away.

"What's with that guy?" David says.

"I have no idea," I say. "And there's no time to find out."

"Got any ideas?" David says.

With nothing concrete, I do what any other astute Hollywood director would do. I buy some time.

"Change in plans, David. We're pushing the finale to tomorrow, so tonight I want you to take yourself and the rest of the crew out for a nice dinner on me."

"What do I tell everyone when they ask why the delay?"

"Make something up. Like Bianca has a big zit on her nose or her gallbladder is acting up. And, if Eric wants to hang back with Bianca, make sure to tell him it's contagious and he can't stay."

David frowns. "A gallbladder attack contagious?"

"I don't know, David! You're the creative one here! Figure something out!"

"Are you sure about this?" David says.

"Absolutely! And put it on Prixie's tab," I say, handing David my corporate credit card. If the company and my career go up in flames, the fire might as well be a three-alarm blaze.

David leaves, and I find Signore Maio just outside her office door again.

"Sorry to bother you again Signora, but, if you could join me in your office, alone?"

Compared to the day she eagerly toured me around, Signore Maio regards me with a suspicious expression.

"Your computer," I say, pointing to Signore Maio's computer. "It wouldn't be connected to any security cameras would it, by any chance?"

Signora Maio's eyes narrow and her tone becomes indignant. "If you're asking me if we spy on our guests, Signorina, I assure you—"

"Oh, no, no. You've completely misunderstood, Signora," I say with a good-hearted chuckle that sounds fake even to my own ears.

"Good. Because I don't want my hotel to be associated with anything scandalous. Do you hear me?"

"Of course. That would never be my intention. I was just hoping that, you know? I could take a look at today's footage?" I say, pointing again at Signora Maio's computer.

Signora Maio takes her sweet time as she considers, precious time I need to find Bianca and bring her back.

Realizing that I have no other option than to sweeten the pot, I say, "You've been more than hospitable. How about I make a little gesture to both you and your staff," I say, putting five fingers in the air.

"A gesture would be nice, but only if you add three more zeros to that number," Signora Maio says.

The woman is a shark, but, with no other choice, I agree to her terms.

Since the footage is time-stamped, it allows me to focus on a slim window of time when it seems most likely that Bianca could have slipped away. I check each view on each camera twice and a third time, but the security camera never catches Bianca exiting her room. Is it possible that Bianca could have climbed down her balcony? I wouldn't put it past her. When Bianca is overwrought, she can act quite feral. But when I check the camera that focuses on the back of the hotel, there's no sign of her in any of that footage either.

For the convenience of its guests, there is usually a private taxi always parked in the circular driveway outside the hotel's main doors. If Bianca did slip out the front door of the hotel, someone would have noticed her leaving.

"Do you mind asking the driver posted at the front of the hotel if he drove a young, attractive brunette somewhere this afternoon?" I ask Signora Maio, as I continue to pour through other footage.

Signora Maio hesitates.

"Very well, I say," putting up another five fingers.

"Plus, three zeros," Signora Maio reminds me.

With a huff, I say, "Okay, okay."

Ten minutes later, Signora Maio returns. "The driver didn't see her," she says.

"How does someone just disappear into thin air?" I say more to myself than Signora Maio.

"Maybe she hasn't disappeared," Signora Maio says like a cat who's just caught a mouse in her mouth but hasn't yet decided to let it go or eat it.

"What are you saying, Signora? That Bianca could still be somewhere in this hotel?"

"It is very plausible, Signorina," she says. "We have so many rooms."

"Signora Maio, do you happen to have a master key for every room in this hotel?"

"Yes, Signorina. We actually have two, in the event that we lose one," she says.

"And how many rooms are there in your hotel?"

"Fifty-six. Why do you ask, Signorina?"

I quickly do the math. "That number, minus the two rooms occupied by Bianca and Jacob, equals fifty-four. Divided into two that is twenty-nine rooms that we would need to search."

"*We*, Signorina?" Signora Maio says.

This time, I don't wait. I spread five fingers out and say, "I know. I know. Add three zeros."

Butterfly Summer

The two of us must work quickly before David and the crew return. Since he just wants me to fall on my face and fail, there's no need to tell Jacob about what we are doing. Knowing him, he'd report me to the legal department for breaking and entering!

I take the even numbered floors and Signore Maio takes the odd. The objective is to be fast, unlocking doors, doing a quick sweep in and out of the room, before moving onto the next one.

After I am done with my first floor, I meet Signora Maio in the elevator. She is red-faced and breathing hard.

"I don't understand," she says. "Why do we have to check all the rooms, even the ones used by the other people on your team?"

"You don't know this girl, Signora. She can be quite tricky. For all I know, this is an inside job and Bianca has convinced someone on the crew to keep her stowed out of sight," I say.

The two of us move on to our next, assigned floors.

Signora Maio gets off at the third floor, but I proceed to the fourth. As I do, my phone starts pinging.

> Sam: *What the hell, Anna? Jacob just called me!*
>
> Avi: *We trusted you on this one! Call us ASAP!!!*

Stupid Jacob! He must've dialed up Sam and Avi the minute he walked away, putting them both in a panic. As I sweep through the first two rooms, I dictate a message:

Anna: *Sorry can't call right now. Kind of busy. Yep, small snafu. Nothing I can't handle. Talking to the people in post to see if they can work with a new timeframe.*

As I move through another two rooms, I dial up Krissy in post. "Hey there! How's sunny L.A. treating you?" I say, in a tone that is totally forced.

Krissy, who is in charge of our post-production team, the team of editors and assistant editors, who take all those whiny-crying, sloppy-kissing, chicken-dancing-sex scenes and turn them into something dramatic and heartfelt.

Krissy, who has been working with me long enough to know when I'm about to ask her for a favor, skips the small talk and jumps right to business. "What's up, Anna? You got some footage coming my way soon?"

"Here's the thing. We've kind of fallen a little behind over here," I say, as I insert the key into the next room. I quickly look around, not forgetting to check under the bed, in the closet, and behind the shower curtain.

"And you need my team to work double time," Krissy says. It's not a question, but a statement, and I can feel Krissy's annoyance through the phone.

"Uhm . . . basically," I say, as I rush to the next room. "Another twenty-four hours. That's all I'm asking for." But even with more time, I'm not sure I'll be able to produce a bride for the show.

Krissy isn't quick to agree, so I use the same strategy I've been using on Signora Maio. "Fine. I'll personally pay your people triple overtime," I say.

"And you'll pay for everyone's dinner," Krissy says.

"Yes. I'll throw dinner in too," I say.

"Make it a good place. We're all tired of ramen," Krissy says.

"Yes. I'll spring for a good place," I promise her.

While all this extortion means that I'm probably working for free right now, I don't have a choice.

When I get off the phone with Krissy, I text Sam and Avi, letting them know that everything with post has been worked out, and I've literally bought us another twenty-four hours.

Again, none of these negotiations will matter a hill of beans if we can't find Bianca.

As I finish searching the fourth floor, I push the button on the elevator. When the doors open, there again is Signora Maio.

I enter the elevator and am about to push the button for my next floor when Signora Maio says, "Don't bother. I found them."

"That's great! Where?" I say. But before Signora Maio answers me, it hits me. "Wait a minute. Who exactly is *them*?"

24.

As Signora Maio uses her master key to unlock Bianca's door, she says, "I know you said not to bother checking her room because it had already been checked, but then I remembered something."

Once we are inside, Bianca's room has been neatened up. The teacups have all been removed, and the bed is freshly made.

Confused, I say to Signora Maio, "Where is she?"

"I remembered that these two rooms are the only ones in the entire hotel that are connected by a door," Signora Maio says, pointing to an additional door I hadn't noticed the first time I was here. "Go ahead, Signorina. I believe you will find her on the other side." At that, Signora Maio, who has more than earned her money today, leaves me alone in the suite.

My legs feel wobbly, but the sensation isn't from all the running I've been doing. Rather, it's from the sudden

realization of what I am about to find on the other side of
the locked door of Bianca's suite.

There is no need for me to use the master key. The door
is unlocked, and the knob turns easily. When I enter the
room, Jacob and Bianca look up at me in surprise.

The two of them are sitting side by side on a couch.
Jacob's arm is draped over Bianca's shoulder, and their
bodies are pushed close together in a way that is
unnecessary given how big the couch is. There's a cup of tea
sitting on the coffee table in front of them. The tea is a
familiar pale-yellow color. It's the same tea I'd seen in the
numerous tea cups previously scattered about Bianca's
room.

As it all finally sinks in, including Signora Maio's
intentional use of the word *them*, Jacob, his smug face
stripped of all its usual arrogance, desperately pleads.
"Please, Anna. Let me explain!"

The sofa where I now sit, the one positioned across
from where Jacob and Bianca are still huddled together, is
upholstered in the same nubby fabric that matches the sofas
in the hotel lobby. As Jacob explains how he and Bianca
realized they were each other's soulmates, I mindlessly rub
my hand over the fabric, as a way to not completely lose my
cool.

"You see, Anna, Bianca and I both love sashimi. But it
goes deeper than that. When we were kids, we both had dogs
named Horatio. I mean, Horatio? Who can deny that this is
kismet," Jacob says.

"Yep, who can deny it," I say, rubbing the cushion so
hard, the friction might start a fire.

My head starts to hurt again, and my eyes drift off in the direction of the balcony as Jacob and Bianca continue to add other things to their in-common list. They both adore sardines and green tea, they were both voted class treasurer in high school, and both of them have an utter contempt for haikus. It's clearly a match made in heaven.

The shutters that lead out to the balcony are open, and in the distance, I notice the top of an ancient umbrella pine. Since we are at least six stories high, the top of the tree is slightly bent. I assume that, over the years, the wind has pushed against it and the tree has learned to adapt by changing its own shape. I, however, am not a tree. I don't adapt quite as easily, despite the theory that sushi, sunsets, and dogs with strange names make for the undisputable fact that two people are meant to be together.

"Bianca has a contract, Jacob. You, of all people, understand the legal dog pile of poop Bianca will find herself in if she doesn't show up on set tomorrow and at least pretend she's excited to be marrying Eric," I say.

Like a two-year-old who's been denied her favorite toy, Bianca throws up her hands and screams. "No, no, no!! I want Jacob!"

Bianca breaks down crying, and Jacob tightens his grip around her shoulders.

"I still don't get the big deal," I say. "You only have to marry Eric for the show. Then, in a week or two, you file an annulment. It's a win-win for everyone!"

Through her sniveling, Bianca says, "It's bad luck to marry someone under false pretenses."

"What about you?" I ask Jacob. "Do you think it's bad luck, too?"

"I want whatever Bianca wants," Jacob says.

I can't believe this. With just a bat of her fake eyelashes, Bianca has single-handedly turned Jacob into a pile of mush.

"Will you help us, Anna?" Jacob says.

"I can't believe this! You want me to tank our whole production company based on something as stupid and unreliable as love?"

Bianca wipes away her tears and turns her big doe eyes on me. "If that's how you really see love, Anna, I kind of feel worse for you than I do for Jacob and me."

Bianca's words feel like a hard slap to the face. While I'm digesting what she's said to me, my phone rings and it's Cheryl.

"You should get that," Jacob says.

"Don't tell me what I should or should not do," I say.

Jacob's eyes get big. He's not used to me snapping at him.

I place my phone, screen side down, next to Jacob's teacup. Because Cheryl's one of those people who never gives up, especially on the orphaned elephants she sponsors in Africa, my phone keeps vibrating, causing the cup to rattle.

When my phone finally stops ringing, it doesn't matter. It's as if Cheryl is sitting there next to me on the couch, urging me to do the right thing.

"I guess we can figure something out," I tell Bianca and Jacob. "Though, I must be out of my mind."

"Really?" Bianca says.

Jacob is over the moon too. "Thank you so much, Anna!" Then, finally sounding like the producer he is, Jacob says, "So, how do we make this happen?"

"I have no idea," I say.

The sun is melting into the bay just as Luca drops me off at my aunt's house. With all the upheaval back at the hotel, my aunt's house has become a surprising sanctuary for me. It swaddles me in peace the minute I walk in. I'd like to think my aunt is here too, also surrounded by the peace and quiet.

As I eat the food Isabella's elves have conveniently dropped off for me, my mind wanders to my visit to the Hotel Gatopardo that morning. One good thing about Jacob and Bianca's drama is that it's left me with little time to think about my own. That short reprieve is over as I sit with my own thoughts.

From what Rosalba said, Delia isn't part of the family hotel. Was that her choice? Or had Paolo's family decided long ago that they didn't want Delia involved? Then why wouldn't she be involved now? Maybe Delia's life took an entirely different course. Maybe she's a mother or even a grandmother. Wherever Delia ended up in her life, seeing Rosalba looking so self-assured, fills me with hope.

I want to tell Cheryl about everything that happened today, and to get her opinion, but when I reach for my phone, I notice Cheryl didn't bother leaving a voice mail after her last call. Remembering how tired she sounded the last time we talked, I give her a break and turn my phone off for the night.

My best thinking happens when I'm walking so I wander from room to room, taking a detour up the stairs to the attic. In the attic, I am shocked to find twenty to thirty boxes, stacked in piles and pushed against the sloping walls. Not knowing that he'd get gravely sick before having a chance to personally sort through my aunt's things, my father's job lands on me.

Butterfly Summer

The first box I open contains some old sweaters. I lift one to my nose and breathe in traces of the familiar laundry detergent my aunt used.

When I lift the lid off the second box, I find a ton of old books, Latin and Ancient Greek mainly. These days, the vast majority of college kids in America choose their major based on how much money they feel they can potentially make, so studying Latin, I imagine, is a real rarity.

A few pages fall out of one book as I flip through it. The glue on the spine has dried out. Eventually, like the people themselves who've read the books, these books will turn to dust too.

I am about to replace the lid when a familiar cover pokes out from under the pile. Reaching in, I pull out my copy of *Marcovaldo*.

Having smelled and tasted some of the most expensive wines in the world, I press the pages to my nose. And there, beneath the layers of time and age, is something far better than anything that can be poured into a glass. It is the scent of glue and paper pulp. This smell, along with the smell of Delia's suntan oil, are the smells I most closely associate with that summer when I was young and in love for the first and the last time in my life.

Is Bianca right about me? Has life really turned me into a bitter old crone, who's lost complete faith in love?

When I get into bed that night, I can't sleep. I turn on the lamp and start reading *Marcovaldo* again. I am surprised by how much of the story I still remember. But this time when I get to the end, my opinion of Marcovaldo is different. Viewing him through the lens of these last forty years, Marcovaldo is not stupid, at all. His willingness to take a chance, despite life not always working out in his favor, is admirable and brave.

I close the book, but I don't turn the bed lamp off right

away. Marcovaldo's unfettered enthusiasm has left a stamp on me, and I know what I have to do. Even though it's way past business hours, I compose an email. Fearing I might lose my nerve, I don't check it for grammatical errors. I just hit send.

25.

"Please explain it to me again," Signore Pisani says. It is eight o'clock in the morning and, for a man accustomed to starting his workday no earlier than ten, he's obviously having a hard time wrapping his head around my sudden change of heart.

"It's simple, Signore. I no longer wish to sell my aunt's house."

"But why now when we've finally found someone?" he says.

Signore Pisani is right to think I'm crazy. Maybe I am. With so many other loose strings in my life, why do I want to add one more complication to my life?

"I will gladly pay you any lost commissions," I say.

Signore Pisani arches his left brow and regards me critically. "Have you spoken to your mother about this?"

In any other part of the world, no lawyer would ever ask a client if they've first conferred with their mother before making a business decision. But in Italy where mothers rate in importance just one step below Jesus and one step above pizza, I am not surprised by Signore Pisani's question.

"She's fine with it," I reassure him, though, at the moment my mother is at home, peacefully sleeping in her bed, clueless to my sudden reverse-course decision. When I do tell her, she's going to flip out. For now, however, I'm putting that conversation on the back burner.

"Very well, but I will need to reach out to her so that she can sign a proxy giving you the authority to decline the sale."

"Uhm . . . Is that really necessary?"

"It is for our records."

Trying to keep my voice steady, I say, "Of course, but she's very busy today. She told me that she's going on the senior bus to Atlantic City, and well, she doesn't like to be disturbed when she's playing the slots."

Signore Pisani eyes me even more suspiciously, but he shrugs, buying me at least, another twenty-four hours.

Signore Pisani sighs. "The buyer will be very disappointed."

Right now, I can't think of the buyer or their feelings because there are other more pressing matters ahead of me.

When I exit the lawyer's office, I turn my phone back on, bracing myself for the onslaught of messages I've intentionally been avoiding. I read the ones from Avi and Sam first. The texts were all written somewhere between three and four o'clock in the morning L.A. time, more proof that the two of them have swapped out their human brains for A.I. brains, helping them to override all basic human necessities such as eating, sleeping and taking a poo.

Butterfly Summer

Avi: *This is really happening today, right?*
Sam: *A little reminder. Your contract is up for renewal at the end of this season.*

Closer to sunrise, I get a text from Jacob.

Jacob: *Namaste, Anna. Just want you to know that I really do appreciate you.*

The next text comes from Bianca. I imagine she wrote it while still in bed, before she plowed into her low-carb breakfast.

Bianca: *You're the best!*

The most cryptic, but easily ignored text comes from David.

David: *We need to talk ASAP. Call me before you get here!!!!!!!*

There is only one text that I don't find annoying:

Isabella: *Buongiorno! Signore Pisani told me about your change of heart. When you can, please call me. I've discovered something very interesting about the buyer.*

I'm about to call Isabella when another text comes in from Luca. In my haste, I'd forgotten to tell Luca to pick me up at Signore Pisani's office.

As I wait for Luca to pick me up near the piazza, I notice two men standing in the fountain's basin. Both are dressed in coveralls. One of the men has a toolbelt around his waist and both of them are pointing to the spot on the fountain where the water would normally be flowing.

When Luca arrives, I jump into the back seat, and another flood of texts blow up my phone. Everyone needs their questions answered ASAP! Unfortunately, my call to Isabella will have to wait.

Luca drops me off in front of the Hotel Ischia Paradiso at a little past 9 a.m. As I'm going through the hotel's main entrance, a hotel employee passes me. He's holding a mop and pushing a rolling bucket filled with putrid smelling water. For whatever reason, the man shoots me a nasty look as we pass each other.

Once I'm inside, a flustered Signora Maio greets me. "Signorina, when I said you could film at my hotel, I did not mean that you and your crew could run around like a pack of wolves!"

"What do you mean? A pack of wolves?" I say.

"Please, follow me," she says.

Signora Maio brings me out to the patio bar. It's a complete shamble. The potted palms are toppled over, and empty wine bottles are strewn everywhere. Someone's bra hangs from one of the blue-striped umbrellas and there are currently two men, dressed in Speedos and goggles, taking turns diving into the pool, attempting to fish out the two lounge chairs that have been dumped at the bottom end.

"What happened?" I ask Signora Maio.

"Your crew came back last night and decided to have a little party. Someone threw up right there under the Oleander, and my staff has been at work, cleaning since they arrived early this morning," she says.

This explains the man with the rolling bucket.

"What is the old saying, Signorina? When the cat's away, the mouse will play?" Signora Maio says.

"Yes, especially when the mice are in possession of my Amex platinum card," I say to myself.

"Scusi?" Signora Maio asks.

"Nothing, nothing, Signora. I'm truly sorry about all of this. I don't know what's gotten into them." This explains why David had been in such a hurry to talk to me.

"You will pay for all the damages. Otherwise, I will not allow you to remain. And even at that, I think I am being very generous," Signora Maio says.

"Of course. My production company will take care of all of it," I say.

The two men in the pool float up to the surface. Both of them have a grip on the end of one lounge chair. According to the call sheet, Signora Maio's staff has just under forty-five minutes until the entire cast and crew is due on set.

"How much to get this all cleaned up in the next twenty-minutes?" I say.

Just as I suspect her to do, Signora Maio raises five fingers in the air. I nod, then watch in dismay as the lounge chair begins to take on water, spiraling in a delicate arabesque, sinking one more time to the bottom of the pool.

Just as I'm about to push the button to call the elevator, David finds me.

"Anna, last night . . . I told them to cut it out. And then, you know . . . things just got out of hand and . . ." he says all spluttery and apologetic.

I place my hands on David's shoulders, look him in the eye and, using a technique Cheryl has often used on me, I say, "Breathe."

David's eyes grow wide. He's not used to me acting this relaxed. David does what I say. He takes a couple of deep gulps of air and his shoulder's relax.

"Better?" I say.

David nods.

"Good. Now, I need you to focus, okay?"

"So, everything is still a go?" David says.

Not wanting to burst his bubble or mine, I say. "Sure."

"Oh my God! That's great!" David says.

The sound of laughter draws my attention to the other side of the lobby to where a bunch of young production assistants stand in a cluster.

"What's that all about?" I say to David.

David turns pale again. "Uhm, yeah . . . Well, last night there was this thing . . . and Eric—"

"Eric? What about Eric?" The last thing I need is another prima donna on my hands.

"It's fine, Anna. Really," David says.

"Oh? Is that why you're having a hard time looking me in the eye?" I tell him.

David looks down at his feet, and I head straight for the group of P.A.s. When one of them sees me, he quickly nudges a girl, who attempts to hide her phone.

"Too late," I say, thrusting out my hand. "Give it over."

With a petrified look on her face, the girl hands her phone to me.

The video they have all been watching is of a shirtless, dancing Eric wearing a spaghetti colander on his head. His dance moves are lewd and aggressive, as he gropes the breasts of the very attractive woman he is dancing with.

"Perfect," I say, shaking my head at Eric's sheer stupidity.

On the Hollywood hierarchal ladder, production assistants rank pretty much on the lowest rung. Many of them are kids, right out of college, looking to get their foot in the door in the industry.

"If I find out that any of you have posted this to social media . . ." I say to the petrified bunch.

All of them shake their heads emphatically, promising they would never do such a thing.

David finds his voice. "Okay! Enough!" he says, clapping his hands. "Take those boxes down to the beach. Now!"

Idiots! All of them! Speaking of idiots, it's time for me to talk to Jacob and Bianca.

As if they are Velcroed together, Jacob and Bianca are again sitting side by side on the sofa. Jacob's T-shirt is wrinkled. Knowing what I know now, I doubt it got that way from his usual strenuous yoga routine.

"Jacob, I'd like to talk to Bianca alone," I say.

Jacob tightens his grip on Bianca's shoulder, and Bianca pats his knee. "It's okay, sweetie. I can handle this," she says.

When Jacob leaves, I turn to Bianca. "Are you sure you don't want to just take the easy way out?"

Bianca shakes her head, her glossy black fringe moving in rhythm. Even when she is being completely bullheaded, Bianca can be quite breathtaking. No wonder Jacob is so attracted to her.

Still not convinced that Little Miss Dulcolax and Mister Sweaty Pits have what it takes to make it last for the long haul, I give Bianca one last chance to change her mind. "You know, it may not seem like a big deal now, but choices do have their consequences. Take it from me. I know firsthand how things can go sideways pretty fast."

Bianca shakes her head. "I know what people say about me. That I'm the girl who cheated her way here."

"Everyone's entitled to a little mistake, sweetie. People will forget all about your little laxative stunt," I say, realizing how ironic that sounds.

"Do you really think I care about other people? The only person's opinion that counts is Jacob's. I need to prove to him that I'm not *that* girl anymore."

Bianca's earnest plea gets me in the gut. But how can I help her when I'm also *that* girl who tends to take the easy way out?

"Please, Anna?"

This is what love does to a person. It makes you believe in the impossible until the inevitable happens and you crash.

Reminding myself to not let my own cynicism get in the way and to be more like Marcovaldo, I say, "Okay. Let's do this." And, because I know he's eavesdropping on the other side of the door, I yell out, "You can come in now, Jacob!"

Jacob steps back into the room. He looks rather sheepish, and his face shows no trace of the hard-nosed executive I once sparred with. "Thank you, Anna," he says.

"You can thank me later, once we know we don't have a complete flop on our hands," I say.

As the door to the suite closes behind me, I hear a torrent of giggles. Who was I with the last time I'd laughed like that? The answer is surprisingly simple, but not one I have time to consider.

Luca is outside, buffing his car with a softy shammy. When he sees me, he quickly runs to open the door for me. Once he is positioned behind the wheel, Luca says, "Where would you like to go, Signorina?"

"Start driving and I'll tell you as we go," I say. It is time to make good on another promise.

26.

O n the drive, I finally get a chance to call Isabella, but it goes straight to voicemail. I begin scrolling through messages, but there's just one person I want to hear from.

Cheryl's been oddly quiet. My text to her this morning had been marked delivered, with no reply back. Because I'm always traveling for work, the miles or the difference in time zones usually makes no difference, but I feel she's pulling away. But why? What I do know is that, without Cheryl, life feels like a tightrope walk without a net.

Luca pulls the car up to the cemetery's arched entrance. "I will wait for you here," he says.

As if the way there is mapped out in my brain, I go to the little shed and fill a bucket with water and walk to my family plot. Other than the addition of my aunt's name, it looks the same.

"I told you I wouldn't forget," I say, speaking to my aunt's spirit. Just as I'd watched her do years ago, I dip a cloth into the bucket of water and clean the marble. The grave is surprisingly clean and there's even a freshly lit candle burning in the brass luminary at the base of the marble slab.

Curious, I wander back to the caretaker's shed, where I find an elderly man, who is meticulously arranging the brooms and rakes.

"Scusi," I say. "Maybe you can help me?"

When I explain who I am, the man beams. His teeth are yellow and rather crooked, but his sweet demeanor shines through in his smile.

"*Una brava persona. Una brava persona*," he says, repeating over and over what a good person my aunt was. Apparently, his children had also been my aunt's pupils. The way Arturo had, this man's appreciation for my aunt also helps to wipe away a little more of the sadness from her death.

"Are you the one who's been taking such good care of my aunt's grave?" I ask the man.

The man nods.

"Thank you so much," I say. "Here, let me offer you a little something."

But as I reach into my pocket, the man waves the money away. "No, no. Someone is already paying me," he explains.

This is odd. If my father made arrangements to care for our family plot, he'd never mentioned it to my mother or me. And what account was the money coming from to pay this man?

"Can you give me the name of the person who is paying you?" I ask.

"Wait and I will go check my records."

He disappears into his shed. After a few minutes, he returns with the kind of spiral notebook I used to take notes in when I was in high school.

The man looks over the columns of names and dates he has methodically noted in pencil. Some of the pages have a dirty fingerprint or two, smearing some of the information.

"Ah, here it is," the man says when he finds my family's last name. "It says here that the cleaning services are being paid for by Signore Generoso," he says.

"Signore Generoso? I've never heard that name before," I say.

Before I can ask the caretaker any more questions, my phone rings. It's Isabella.

"Scusi," I say to the man, as I take a few steps away, in the direction of the arched entrance.

Before I can even say hello, Isabella launches breathlessly into what it is she wants to tell me.

"I've discovered something new, Signorina, but I hope you don't think badly of me. You see, today, when Signore Pisani went to the café for his afternoon coffee, I searched through his file cabinet."

Still thinking her talents are being somewhat wasted on this small island, I say, "Don't worry, Isabella. Whatever you have to say is between you and me."

My reassurance is enough to open the flood gates for what Isabella has to say. "You see, Signorina, I realized in the end, that it is not the filing system that is faulty, but my own logic. And once I changed my view, it all became extremely clear to me what it was that I was missing out on seeing!"

I check my watch. The rehearsal will be starting soon and I need to speed Isabella along. "What did you find exactly?"

"The original name on the estate," Isabella says, with a little skip in her voice.

My gaze falls back on the caretaker. He's resumed his task of organizing his brooms and rakes. Just as Isabella needed to change her own perspective, I realize that I haven't been focused on the whole picture, just the smaller details.

"Is the name of the estate Generoso, by any chance?" I ask Isabella.

The phone goes silent for a few seconds. "Yes, Signorina. How did you know? Is that why you asked me and Luca about the gas station?"

"I'm confused. Who said anything about the gas station?"

"Because the owner of the gas station was Gaetano Generoso. The same name that is on the estate," Isabella explains.

A memory flashes in my mind of Signore Chiachiaron sprinting to action when my aunt needed him most and the sweet way he called her name. Mareee! Mareee!

Signore Chiachiaron had been in love with my aunt. Why had I failed to notice something so obvious?

"When did he die?" I ask Isabella.

"A year ago," she says.

"So, obviously he's not the one buying the property."

"No and, apparently, he never married and he had no children, so a Trustee was assigned to manage his estate and to execute his will."

"And that's the person who doesn't want their identity revealed," I say.

"Exactly!" Isabella says. "And I've read over all the documents. The person is only referred to as the Trustee, nothing else. It's all been very unusual and hush-hush."

I look at the time. "I can't tell you how much I appreciate this, Isabella. Unfortunately, the rest of this will have to wait because I'm kind of on a tight schedule."

Butterfly Summer

"I understand, Signorina," Isabella says.

After I hang up with Isabella, I find Luca. As promised, he is waiting for me outside the cemetery entrance. "Where to next, Signorina?" he says.

While my phone is blowing up with messages and I really should be getting back to the hotel, I say, "There's one more stop I need to make, Luca."

Luca sits in the driver's seat while I sit in the back, staring quietly out the window. We have been parked already for a half-hour. Whether he is just too polite to say anything or he's just come to accept that I am some weird American lady, Luca doesn't ask me why we have suddenly found ourselves parked in front of a grocery store in Piazza Bagni.

The store has a new name - Supermercato Supreme – which makes it sound fancier than it looks. The store is a lot more rundown than I remember it with a big, metal, garbage dumpster and a bunch of shopping carts sitting scattered idly in front of the entrance.

Beyond all those abandoned shopping carts, I imagine the way I wished that night had gone. Like an epic Hollywood movie, I envision Marco, still dressed in his wedding suit and white Capezios swooping in to save Delia as she restocked bags of frozen peas. Of course, Delia being Delia would have put up some resistance. But after Marco explained that it was me who'd put him up to it, Delia would see that love was my only motive and she would relent.

"Is everything okay, Signorina?" Luca says. "If you are hungry, there are much better grocery stores I can take you to if you like."

Hungry? Yes. I am starving, but not for food.

"No, thank you, Luca. We can go," I say, because even if Delia and I never got to have our happily-ever-after, I can try to give another couple theirs.

27.

As we make our way back to the Hotel Ischia Paradiso I set in motion a strategy that I pray will work.

I send out a fury of texts. Once I know I have done all I can do, I sit back in my seat, my mind returning to Signore Chiachiaron, whose name I now realize is Gaetano Generoso. For as long as I can recall, the gas station had always been there. But had Gaetano Generoso always worked there? Is that how he'd first set eyes on my aunt? Or were they friends from school?

When she's not obsessing over elephants, Cheryl's viewing preferences lean toward romantic comedies. Since I'm more of a Sci-Fi kind of gal, it's something I endlessly tease her about. With a few minutes to spare before we arrive at the hotel, there's no one else I rather share this latest romantic tidbit of news with than Cheryl.

My call goes straight to voicemail and my uneasiness turns to dread. Maybe it's Cheryl, not Jacob, who's had one foot out the door this entire time.

My phone rings and my heart skips in my chest hoping it's Cheryl calling me back. Instead, it's Isabella. In the background, I hear the sound of traffic humming by.

"Where are you?" I say.

"In the piazza. I came outside so Signore Pisani couldn't hear our conversation," she explains.

"Is everything okay?"

"It is more than okay, Signorina. The Trustee for the Generoso estate showed up at Signore Pisani's office. She is very upset about the fact that you have changed your mind about selling."

"She? So, the Trustee of the estate is a woman?"

"Yes, but that is not the only interesting fact, Signorina. The woman happens to have the same last name as your friend," Isabella says, just as Luca pulls our car up to the front entrance of the hotel.

A whooshing sound fills my ears as my racing heart floods my ears with blood. "Oh, my God, Isabella. Is it Delia?" I ask Isabella.

"No, Signorina. Only the last name is the same. Plus, this woman is much too young to be your friend."

"I don't understand. How were you able to learn her name?" I ask her.

"Signore Pisani asked me to make a copy of the woman's driver's license for the file. When I saw it, I couldn't believe it either."

I am at a complete loss for words. What could possibly be the connection between Delia, this woman and Signore Generoso?

"Signorina? Are you still there? Are you okay?" Isabella says.

"Yes. I'm okay," I tell Isabella. Outside the car window, I watch as crew members push trolly carts loaded with equipment in the direction of the beach.

"Listen, Isabella, I'm going to be a little out of pocket for the rest of the day."

"Out of pocket?" Isabella says.

"What I mean is I won't be able to talk again until I finish up here. After that, I will address whatever it is that is going on there. Ok?"

"Ok, Signorina. Good luck!" Isabella.

"Thank you, Isabella. I'll need all the luck I can get," I say.

As I make my way down to the beach, my head is still spinning, so much so that I don't immediately notice how the beach has been completely transformed.

David rushes up to me. "Whaddaya think? Whaddaya think?" he says, accidently kicking up sand. The guy is completely wired, making me wonder whether he's had more than two hours of sleep over the last forty-eight hours.

"It's amazing," I say, finally taking it all in. The plain slip of sand Signora Maio had previously shown me has now been turned into a romantic oasis. The rail on the stone staircase is draped with yards of tulle fabric, interspersed with baby's breath and dozens of yellow and pink roses. Hundreds of rose petals create a makeshift path, which leads to an ornately woven pergola. Originally intended for the Türkiye location, the pergola had been custom designed by our design staff. To make the branches more pliable, the team needed to first soak each piece in a solution of elecampane oil before building the structure.

Elecampane oil is rare. So, when the bill came, Avi nearly flipped his yarmulke. "Why do two non-Jews need such an expensive chuppah?" he'd said.

Because I was focused more on production value, than the actual value of love, I said, "Ari, love has to look convincing to be convincing."

Cheryl happened to be taking notes at the meeting that day. Looking for reinforcement, I'd said, "Isn't that right, Cheryl?" To which, Cheryl yawned.

Cheryl's underwhelming enthusiasm aside, Avi gave in, and I got my pergola. I also got the hundreds of floating tealights that a group of underwater divers are now in the process of lighting. The only thing left for me to do is pray.

Out of sheer necessity, I've had to clue David in on my plan too. This is why his anxiety is running rampant and he just won't shut up.

"Everything is set up. Are all the . . . you know . . . key players ready for this? Oh, my God. I can't believe we're doing this without rehearsing it first, but I completely get it!"

David and I both know that, in order for things to work out, an element of surprise is absolutely necessary.

On my way back to the hotel, I called David. "You know that production assistant who took the video of Eric? I need to talk to her now!"

The production assistant's name is Alexa. I could tell she was intimidated by me because, when she said, "You want me to what?" her voice squeaked.

Not wanting to spook the poor kid, I said, "Alexa, I would very much appreciate it if you could post that video to every social medial outlet out there and do it quickly."

Alexa's fear morphed into a nervous giggle. "Is this some kind of set-up?"

"Listen, Alexa. Do this for me, and I'll make sure you get a full-time position on next season's show, okay?" I said.

The promise of a full-time gig made Alexa and I lifelong friends.

Butterfly Summer

I scroll through the comments on every official *Bride-to-Be* social media page. Just as I'd hoped, the anonymous post showing Eric's wine-fueled night is starting to go viral. While public opinion is split, the important thing is that people are expressing those opinions *a lot*.

With the ground swell created, it is now time to ride the momentum.

"Roll camera!" I yell.

Jacob and I stand next to each other, just out of frame.

"Would you please stop fidgeting." I talk in a whisper, cautious for any hot mic that might be lurking.

"What if Bianca comes off as a jerk? She'll be devastated, and she may not be able to forgive me," Jacob says.

"Bianca is hardly Mother Theresa."

In his pre-Bianca days, Jacob would have easily come back at me with a snarky remark, but love has reduced the poor guy to mush. He just stands there ringing his hands.

Maybe it's this new revelation about Signore Chiachiaron's feelings for my aunt that makes me more sympathetic toward Jacob, but I say, "Don't worry, Jacob. If it doesn't work out, you'll find a way to survive. We all do."

"Don't you understand, Anna? Love is the only reason to live. Without it, there is no survival."

Jacob's words hit me like a landslide. After Delia, I'd survived my heartache by retreating into my protective shell. Because of that choice, I've missed out on a lot of life.

A quintet made up of three violins, a cello and one piccolo start to play. Taking a brief break from the comments pouring in on social media, I look out at the sea.

The tealights are all lit, their twinkling flames reflecting off the water.

I remember that day in my aunt's kitchen, as she sang. *"Quando sei innamorato, tuo sorriso brilla come le stelle.* When you're in love, your smile shines bright like the stars."

That summer hadn't been filled entirely with sadness. There'd been happy moments too. And while we'd never said the words, I loved my aunt, and I knew she loved me.

Jacob bites his cuticles as Eric, handsome in his Brioni suit, stands next to Arnold, the witty officiant, who's been officiating every wedding from season one. Arnold is a fan favorite and he's also in on my scheme.

A monitor, which is connected to the fancy Red Dragon cameras that also cost a mint, is positioned in front of me. Before bringing him on set, I'd made sure that Alexa alerted Eric to all the comments being posted about him on social media. The girl has to cut her teeth somewhere, especially since she'll be working with us full-time next year. And from what I can tell from the monitor, Alexa's subtle coaching seems to be working. The usual easygoing Eric begins showing signs of stress. His brow is furrowed and a little trickle of sweat runs down the side of his face.

The piccolo hits a deliciously high note and, a second later, right on cue, Bianca appears at the top of the staircase. Next to me, Jacob chokes back tears.

"Keep it together," I tell him.

With choreographed precision, camera one focuses on Bianca, while camera two closes in on Eric, creating a split screen effect for the audience. Bianca's face reads innocent, purposely clueless. While Eric looks guilt-ridden. The impression of a sailboat merrily, sailing along, naively unaware of the storm raging toward it hits just the right note.

Bianca begins making her way down the stairs.

Surreptitiously, I scroll through the latest batch of comments. The responses coming in are a mixed bag.

In Camp Bianca, we have comments like:

> *Dump that mother*#@'s ass.*
> *Boss babes don't play that.*
> *Eric's gotta cut those carbs.*
> *#donewithspaghetti*

Meanwhile, in Camp Eric, the comments are a bit more sympathetic:

> *Give the guy a break!*
> *A man's gotta eat* 😊
> *#thatsamore*

Even though the audience is still divided, the back and forth should translate into ratings gold. At least, I hope it does.

With only a few steps to go toward the pergola, Bianca's performance is on par with Meryl Streep. Her face remains serene and confident, with absolutely no hint of what's to come.

I whisper to Jacob. "She's really good."

"She's a star," he says, swallowing back another bath of tears.

His comment makes me think about the tealights off the beach. What if the kind of love, powerful enough to summon down the stars, really did exist?

Bianca reaches the pergola. What typically comes next is that the groom-to-be will put his hand out to his bride. It's a small, welcoming gesture meant to convey the groom-to-be's ecstasy for being the last man standing. But, today, Eric does not put his hand out. In fact, he doesn't even make eye contact with Bianca. Instead, he keeps his hands glued to his sides. Bianca, who needs no coaching, appears confused. She clutches her bouquet, a subtle tightness settling in her jaw that shows up clearly on the monitor.

Arnold glances at Bianca and Eric. His slightly surprised expression confirms what the audience already knows. Something is really off between these two.

As Arnold has done in all the previous seasons, he begins with a brief monologue. "Bianca and Eric, let me first start by saying that it has been a personal honor to watch the love between the two of you grow," he says.

Camera three draws in for a close-up of Bianca's gown. Vera has really outdone herself this time. The gown is backless, tapering down to the top of Bianca's waist. Something else the camera picks up is how Bianca's spine stiffens when she hears Arnold say these things.

I hold my breath. This is the defining moment when my plan either works, or I will be forced into some kind of temp work, a Hollywood leper.

Then it happens. Eric unglues one of his hands from his side and, to Arnold, says, "Please. Can you give Bianca and me a moment?"

Arnold's face drops. To demonstrate to the audience that he's now in unchartered waters, Arnold looks around, as if he's seeking guidance from the director. Apparently, Arnold is a method actor, because this isn't anything we've discussed and none of us are prepared for this.

From his director's chair, David shoots me a *WTF* look. I quickly reply with a roll of my hands, letting him know to just go with it.

Since Bianca has historically been painted as a total freak-out girl, it makes total sense when Arnold says, "Are you sure you're okay with this?"

Bianca nods and Arnold steps away. It's the perfect dose of authenticity the performance needs, and one I will be compensating Arnold heavily for come bonus time.

David has excellent instincts. He directs a camera to zoom in on Eric. This is for the money shot. Eric, whose college football career ended when he broke his arm doing a handstand on a beer keg, will either fumble the ball or score.

"Bianca, this isn't the way I imagined this moment would go," Eric says.

Off in the corner, Alexa stands, casually holding her phone at waist level. Normally, cellphones are off-limits on set, but I've specifically directed Alexa to catch all the behind-the-scenes stuff.

"Oh, Eric," Bianca says, placing her finger gently on Eric's lips to stop him from going any further. "I know what you're going to say," Bianca says.

Because Bianca is caught up in her performance, she forgets to drop her hand from Eric's mouth.

"You do?" Eric says, his words warbled.

"I know what happened last night, at the restaurant, with the waitress," Bianca says. "And it's okay, Eric. I forgive you."

This is the moment when it can all go sideways. When Eric, realizes he's been a real lout but a lout that wants to do the right thing. When he forgets what people are saying about him on social media and professes his undying love to a woman he was never really into in the first place.

At the edge of my vision, one of the grips pushes a cameraman, sitting in a dolly that runs on a track, toward Bianca. As he does this, a tight close up of Bianca's face appears on my monitor. I make a mental note to tell Krissy that, when she gets the footage, she should add a couple of sparkly halo filters behind Bianca's head, giving her a saintly glow.

Bianca looks at Eric endearingly, without any trace of judgement or anger on her face. Even though sixty-one percent of voters think Bianca should run Eric's private parts through a pasta maker right now, I am starting to think that this isn't going to pan out the way I want it to.

"Eric, I knew from the moment I met you that we were the same kind of people, frail creatures. I've made mistakes too and done things without thinking how it might hurt the other person," Bianca says.

Next to me, Jacob lets out a big sigh. While Bianca's stream of conscious rant will never win her an Emmy, it comes off as heartfelt and sincere. It also plucks at my own heartstrings in a way that surprises me.

"What a dear, dear, dear, dear heart you are," Eric says. Eric bites his lip. "But, I'm sorry, Bianca. You're just way too good for me."

The cameraman pushes in even closer on Bianca's face. Her bottom lip quivers.

Eric takes a step, but before he goes, he looks meaningfully in Bianca's eyes. "I will work hard to be a better man, Bianca. And, if our destinies should cross paths ever again, just maybe you'll consider taking me back?"

With that Eric walks off set and David yells, "Cut!"

Instead of being happy with the results, Jacob glares at me. "What the hell was all that about crossing paths?"

Relieved that it's all over, I laugh.

Still enraged, Jacob says, "What's so funny?"

"Eric's not as stupid as we thought. I think he's just set himself up for a sequel."

"Sequel, my butt," Jacob says.

"Oh, come on, Jacob. Does it matter? You got what you wanted, didn't you? Bianca's happy, so you can be happy too, right?"

Remembering the whole point of this charade, Jacob smiles. "Yes, I did," he says.

Arnold walks back on set. He puts his arms around Bianca, who is doing an excellent job of wallowing in her heartbreak. Alexa continues to stand in the wings, recording every gut-wrenching sob.

What she fails to catch, however, is the one brief moment when Bianca raises her head from Arnold's shoulder and she locks eyes lovingly with Jacob.

28.

As Luca drives me back to my aunt's, the texts start pouring in.

Sam: *Why aren't you picking up your phone? There was a mole on set who leaked video to social media! It's going viral, and the network is pissed!*

Avi: *What the hell is going on over there? The network is threatening to sue! Why the hell aren't you picking up your phone!!!*

Sam: *Where's Jacob?*

Avi: *Now Jacob's not answering. What is wrong with you two? Is this some kind of coup?*

Jacob and Bianca: *Thank you!!! XOXOXO*

The only text I am happy to see is the next one.

> Cheryl: *Word on the street is you're stirring up trouble.*
> Anna: *Well, you know. Go big or go home* 😊
> Cheryl: *From what I've heard you're not selling the house. Does that mean you're not coming home?*
> Anna: *I guess you've been talking to my mother.*

The next text answers my question.

> Mom: *Signore Pisani said you changed your mind about selling the house? Are you crazy?*

Though I'm not pleased the man went over my head, at least Signore Pisani has saved me the hassle.

My response to my mother is the whishy-washiest answer that I can give – a non-committal thumbs up.

As for Cheryl, I toggle back and forth on what I should say until I decide I'll talk to her when I have some real answers.

The day's events have left me feeling so edgy that I can really use a bit of exercise. "Luca, would you please drop me off in the piazza instead of taking me straight home?"

"Certainly, Signorina," Luca says.

As Luca drives away, I take a walk around the piazza, finally settling myself on the edge of the fountain. At this time of night, during the off season, everything is quiet because of the cold. Most people would rather sit at home, snug with their families, eating dinner or watching T.V. For me, it's not the cold that makes me seek out comfort. Rather, it's the sharp pang of loneliness that causes me to reach for my phone.

Hoping I'm not interrupting Isabella's family time, I text her.

> Anna: *The driver's license you copied? Do you remember the address?*
> Isabella: *Yes. Would you like it?*

My fingers hover over my phone and, taking a deep breath, I text.

> Anna: *Please text it to Luca in the morning.*
> Isabella: *I will do that. Buonanotte, Signorina. Sleep well.*

As I make my way in the direction of my aunt's house, I doubt I'll get any sleep tonight.

Just as he has every morning, Luca is outside waiting for me. Today, however, he has not opened the car door.

"I thought you might prefer to walk, Signorina. Since it is only two short blocks," Luca says, pointing in the direction of the maze of narrow streets where Delia and I once wandered.

How can it be? Two blocks? Is it possible that Delia's been under my nose this entire time? For all I know, we've passed each other, neither one recognizing the other.

"Yes, Luca. I would prefer that."

I find the house with relative ease. Its bright blue door stands out amongst its more demure neighbors. The cheeriness of the door, I hope, is a sign that, despite me, Delia has managed to have a happy life.

I knock and when the door opens, a young woman, with familiar dark curls and large, brown eyes, stands on the other side.

"Buongiorno," the young woman says. While she may resemble Delia, just as Isabella said, she is a good twenty years younger. She is also dressed far more conservatively than Delia would have ever dressed, in crisp, linen pants and a tailored button-down shirt. Delia wouldn't be caught dead wearing something this prim and proper. At least, the Delia I remember.

I manage to calm my heart, which has been on the verge of jumping out of my mouth. "My name is Anna Monti," I say.

Before I can say anything further, the woman flashes me a friendly smile. "I had a feeling you would eventually find me. Please. Come in."

The woman's home would be what an L.A. realtor might call a bungalow. Small, but quaint, and as neat and breezy as the woman's linen outfit.

My eyes skip around the house, looking for clues. "You live here alone?" I say, trying to sound as nonchalant as possible.

"It's just me and Alfredo," the woman explains. On cue, a tiger-tailed cat comes out from behind the couch. It rubs its body against my leg in greeting.

"Say hello to our friend, Alfredo," the woman says to the cat. "Please, Signorina, have a seat. Would you like a coffee? I've just brewed a fresh pot."

I say no to the offer of coffee, but I do sit down.

"I suppose you've come to tell me in person that you no longer want to sell your house?" the woman says.

"Yes, I'm very sorry," I say. "My aunt's house means a lot to me. And now that I'm back here, I'm finding it difficult to part with. I hope you can understand."

"Yes. Professoressa Maria Monti was a wonderful woman and a very dedicated teacher who really cared about her students."

When the woman smiles, she smiles with her entire mouth in a way that is also breathtakingly familiar. But who is this woman? And what is her connection to Delia?

"If you don't mind me asking, how is it that you know my aunt? You're obviously much too young to be one of her former students," I say.

"You're right, but my aunts spoke of her all the time,"

"Your aunts?"

"Yes. My Zia Rosalba and my Zia Delia," she says.

Delia's niece! That toothy smile! It suddenly makes sense. "You're Marco's daughter?"

"Yes. I am Marina."

The idea that Marco is now a grown man with a grown daughter of his own is an idea that's both beautiful and daunting. It again cements in my brain the realization of how much time has passed and how little time I have ahead of me to make things right.

"Here, let me show you something," Marina says.

A low, wooden trunk is pushed against the wall. Marina lifts the top off and begins rummaging through it. She pulls out a photo album and comes to sit down next to me on the couch. She flips through a few pages, finds the photo she wants, and points to it.

"See. That is my Zia Rosalba and your aunt on the day of my Zia's graduation," Marina says.

In the photo, Rosalba, a few years before she would marry that dope, Paolo, stands proudly next to my aunt. While it's a sweet photo, for me, it also brings up a lot of sadness.

"Nice," I say, though I don't see why Marina finds it necessary to show me this photo.

"Wait, there is one more," Marina says.

Marina flips over another handful of pages and points to another photo. "And here is your aunt with my Zia Delia at her high school graduation," she says.

In this second photo, my aunt's hair is grayer compared to the last time I saw her. And next to her is a slightly taller, and slightly less round in the face, Delia. But what shocks me the most is what Delia has in her hand. It's her diploma. The look of pride on both of their faces pops right off the page.

Unable to contain the shock in my voice, I say, "Your aunt Delia graduated from high school?"

"Ah, so you do remember my aunt well?" Marina laughs, exposing again the large teeth she inherited from her father. "Oh, yes. She graduated. To this day, my father tells the story of how he literally had to drag his sister back to your aunt's house and sit with her until she completed her lessons."

Tracing the photo with my hand, I say, "But I thought my aunt gave up," I say.

Marina misinterprets what I mean by *giving up*. With compassion in her voice, she says, "It is very sad what happened with your aunt, Signorina. But that should not overshadow the fact that, when it came to her students, she was a devoted teacher."

This photo is proof that I am not responsible for destroying Delia's life. In my chest, my wounded heart is knit back together.

But there are still so many unanswered questions. "Your aunt Delia? Does she still live in Ischia?" I say, forcing myself to sound as casual and cool as possible.

Marina places the photo album down and with a heaviness in her voice, says, "I'm sorry, Signorina. I thought you knew."

"Knew what?" But the moment the question leaves my tongue, I know that the real pain of saying goodbye has begun.

Marina tells me about the car accident, as I continue to stare at the photo album which is still turned to the page of Delia on her graduation day. All the pain that I have not wanted to feel for all these years, finally demands accountability, and the tears begin to flow down my cheeks.

"Are you okay, Signorina? Here, let me get you some ice water," Marina says.

Marina returns with the water and a box of tissues.

"You and my aunt were friends?" Marina says.

I dry my tears and blow my nose. "Yes. I was seventeen and your aunt Delia was fifteen."

"Seventeen and fifteen. Those are fun ages to be, especially in Ischia," Marina says.

"Well, your aunt was the fun one. I just sort of followed her," I say.

Marina laughs. "That sounds just like her. I can tell you knew her very well."

"Not well enough," I say, sadly.

"Tell me what you remember about her," Marina urges me. The resemblance to her father is uncanny, but what she's inherited most from Marco is his gentleness.

"Well, as you already know, she could be stubborn, like a mule."

Marina laughs, which makes me laugh a little too. "What else did you love about her?"

"I loved when she danced. She would sort of do this thing with her arms . . ."

233

"Spread them out? Like a butterfly?" Marina says, finishing my thoughts.

My breath catches in my throat and I nod.

"It is very faint because I was so young, but I do remember her dancing like that," Marina says.

Marina and I sit quietly for a moment. It's as if the two of us are remembering what we've lost, but also those things that will never be taken away from us.

29.

"So, now that I know who your aunt and father are, how in the world did you become the Trustee for Signore Generoso's estate?" I say.

"It is kind of a long, complicated story," Marina explains.

"Marina, I work in Hollywood where long and complicated stories are the norm," I say.

After Delia graduated from high school, she went to work in a nursing home. "My father and Zia Rosalba thought she was crazy. They tried convincing her to come work with them in Zio Paolo's hotel. But Zia Delia hated him. Besides, she always had her own vision for what she wanted for her life," Marina says.

Knowing that Delia never lost that essential part of herself brings me immense joy. I also love that Delia refused to work under Paolo's controlling thumb.

"My aunt loved working with the elderly. She'd been working at this one particular nursing home for almost ten years when Signore Generoso became a resident. I guess the two of them had known each other in passing, but during this time they became quite close. They liked to play cards and the two of them would try to outdo each other with who could tell the best joke."

I recall how Delia and Signore Generoso would wave to each other. It makes it easy to picture how the two of them might become close.

"It was a year before Aunt Delia's death that Signore Generoso called his lawyer in to put his estate in order. Since he had no children of his own, he told my aunt that he wanted her to be his sole heir. Little did he know that she would die before him."

Hearing Marina talk about Delia's passing still feels so surreal, but I still don't understand what my aunt's house has to do with any of this.

"So, Signore Generoso left his estate to your aunt?" I ask.

"He wanted to, but Zia Delia refused."

"Refused?"

"Yes. Besides being stubborn, Zia Delia was also quite proud. But you see, Signore Generoso had once confided in Zia Delia his feelings for the Professoressa. That is how she came up with the idea."

"The idea to buy my aunt's house?"

"Yes. She wanted to honor the Professoressa by establishing a foundation for people who are struggling," Marina says.

"Struggling with mental illness you mean," I say.

"Yes, Signorina."

"It's okay, Marina. I know how my aunt died. It's sad, but it's also the truth and I'm not ashamed of speaking the truth anymore."

Marina nods. In her eyes, I recognize the look of

admiration. However, her admiration is not something I'm able to accept yet.

"Zia Delia also knew how secrets hurt people. She wanted to create a place where people could feel safe to express their feelings and be accepted for who they truly are."

Goosebumps prickle my skin. Speaking through her niece, it's as if Delia is wrapping her arms around me, enveloping me in her warmth and peace.

If Delia is forgiving me, maybe it's time I forgive myself. "No more brutta figura," I say, more to myself.

"Exactly," Marina says again.

Like books being reshelved, these new facts, with the exception of one thing, find a new place in my heart and head. "There's only one thing," I say. "Why keep the purchase of the house a secret?"

Marina shrugs. "I honestly can't say. It was a provision of the estate and, when I took my aunt's place, my job was to follow what the estate tells me to do."

"I see," I say, as I come to accept that, in life, there will always be some lingering questions that can never be tied up neatly in the way we would like.

"So, what do you think, Signorina? Do you still plan to keep your aunt's house? Or have you changed your mind?"

Butterfly Summer

I tell Avi and Sam that I won't be back for another week. Instead of arguing or yelling, both of them are beyond agreeable.

Sam: *Take as much time as you like!*
Avi: *Planning a shindig at Nobu's for when you get back! Bring home a big appetite!*

Their reaction is in large part due to the ratings for Bianca and Eric's finale. Bianca's sob story has earned us ten more seasons, and Avi and Sam are already working on a spin-off for Eric. Redemption is a hot-ticket item in reality TV, so Sam and Avi are jumping on the bandwagon.

Informing Avi and Sam about my delayed return is one thing. Summoning up the courage to tell Cheryl is another thing.

When Cheryl finally picks up the phone, there are a few more bumps in our conversation.

"I just need another week to clear things up here. Then I'm coming home," I tell her.

As it would happen every so often on those Sunday calls to my aunt, it appears as if the line drops.

"Hello? Cheryl? Did you hear me? I said I'll be home soon."

But it's not the connection. It's Cheryl. She's crying.

"Are you okay? What did I say?" I say.

"Nothing," Cheryl says, sniffing. "I'm just happy because . . . because . . ."

Because I want to be like that silly Marcovaldo who is brave enough to take a chance, I do something I haven't done in a long time. I express the deepest truth in my heart.

"I love you too, Cheryl," I say. "And I promise I will make up for all the lost time."

"I love you too," Cheryl says, in between tears. If it came down to a contest between Bianca and Cheryl, my sweet Cheryl would be the hands down winner for best sobber.

After I get off the phone with Cheryl, Luca texts me. He and Marina are downstairs waiting to take me to Signore Pisani's office where Marina and I will sign the papers, confirming the sale of my aunt's house to the Gaetano Generoso estate.

There is an additional set of papers that I've asked Signore Pisani to draw up, as well. These papers will establish the Maria Monti Center for Wellbeing.

As I get in the car, Marina is already in the backseat waiting for me. "I asked Isabella if she could look into getting the final approval from the town. You know, in Italy, these things take a while," Marina says.

"Italy isn't exactly known for being speedy," I say, which makes the both of us laugh.

Before Luca starts the car, Marina says, "Are you sure you want to do this?"

Even though I will never know if Delia loved me the same way I loved her, knowing that I can be part of her dream means that we will always be connected.

"Absolutely," I say. And as the co-trustee of the Maria Monti Center, I've already committed my share of the sale of the house to the foundation, along with part of the bonus I'll be getting from the biggest ratings boost in *Bride-to-Be* history. The other half of my bonus will pay for a trip for two to an elephant sanctuary in Africa.

In addition to Africa, Cheryl and I will be coming back to Ischia next summer for a wedding. Not ours. Bianca and Jacob's.

"Ready?" Luca says.

Butterfly Summer

"Ready," I say.

When we park near the piazza, I look out the car window. I can't believe my eyes! The fountain is again gushing, the basin bubbling and full with fresh, sparkling water.

TONI DE PALMA

AUTHOR'S NOTE

While *Butterfly Summer* is a work of fiction, the story does incorporate a true event, the loss of my own A'zi by suicide. My aunt was a brilliant woman, who dedicated her life to her students. It is my hope that, by writing this book, I have paid tribute to her memory. While awareness around mental illness has evolved since my aunt's passing, and better medications and treatments are available, there is still much more to do. Every person suffering has the right to respect, understanding, and care because, when one person takes their lives, it has a ripple effect and individuals, families and whole societies are robbed of that person's beautiful light and potential.

If you're going through a tough time
and can use emotional support
or know someone who is,
please call or text
The National Suicide & Crisis Lifeline at 988.
Just those three numbers. 988.

BEHIND THE SCENES

While I consider myself a fiction writer, every novel I've ever written has been inspired by an actual life event that I've personally experienced or by some type of human conundrum that I am grappling with. For *Butterfly Summer*, both of these things are true; the event being my aunt's suicide and the long-standing feeling of regret, that perhaps, I could have done more to prevent it.

Writing *Butterfly Summer*, which is a mingling of truth and Anna's fictious story, gave me a chance to reflect on how one's regrets over past choices can have an impact on one's future. As you can imagine, more than a few tears were shed in the remembering. However, no one was more surprised than I was when some of those tears did not spring from sadness but rather love and gratitude for those beautiful days my aunt and I spent together on the most beautiful island on Earth.

TONI DE PALMA
PICTURES – PAST AND PRESENT

Here are a few pictures from my time spent in Ischia. While some of the images are a bit fuzzy, the memories remain clear in my mind and in my heart.

My dad and I on the main corso circa 1969.
This is where I imagine Anna and Delia (with poor Marco picking up the rear) walking. The water is to the right and the port of Casamicciola is in the not too far distance.

My aunt and I on San Montano beach. She is so protective of me in this photo.

Having fun and trying to get my aunt to laugh.

All grown up. I'm close to Anna's age in this photo.
Looks like I'm reflecting on the
past and also dreaming of the future.

ACKNOWLEDGEMENTS

A big thanks goes to the following people for all your support and encouragement:

Thank you to my publisher and editor, Maer Wilson, who immediately said "why not?" when I asked her if she would consider creating a new imprint for her flagship publishing company, Ellysian Press. In creating Evoke Press, Maer has taught me an invaluable life lesson – you should always ask for what you want, because sometimes you just might get it! Through the editing process, she also taught me to trust my first impulse and have faith, another invaluable life lesson.

Thank you to my first readers, Anne Dudajek Fogarty-Santomauro, Laurie Caudle, Julia De Palma, and Stella Mastellone, for seeing the potential in this story and for pushing me past the finish line.

Thank you to Alyce Slotnick Weiss for allowing me to borrow her name and for being such a good friend, not just on the page, but in real life too.

Un bacio grande goes to Ellen Verde, whose own Ischia journey has inspired me so much. Thank you, Ellen, for obtaining my grandparent's documents in Ischia so that I can pursue my dream of Italian Citizenship. Ellen, your heart is as warm and beautiful as an Ischia sunset.

Thank you to Sara Cricco for answering my Italian grammar questions. I hope to meet you in person some day!

Mena Cuomo, what a gift to discover a cousin I never knew I had! Mena, thank you for sharing your memories of

Zia Maria. Knowing how much she was admired and loved by her students is a gift I am truly grateful for. Your words have healed me more than you will ever know.

Thank you to all the *Ischitani*. When I close my eyes, I can hear your musical voices echoing in my heart.

Thank you to my husband, son, and my beautiful mom. Having the three of you in my corner gives me the courage I need to stretch my wings.

And, finally, I thank my dog, Chester, who was my one true constant when it was just me, my computer and the musings in my head.

ABOUT THE AUTHOR

Toni De Palma is the award-winning author of *Under the Banyan Tree,* which was selected as a Kirkus New Voices Pick and a New York Public Library Book for the Teen Age.

Her other Y.A. works include *The Devil's Triangle* and *Jeremy Owl.*

Toni earned her M.F.A. in Writing for Children and Young Adults from Vermont College She is the recipient of a fellowship from the New Jersey Arts Council. Toni's interests extend to all areas of writing.

In recent years, Toni has widened her interests into filmmaking and has successfully produced, written and directed *Marty's Calling*, which was chosen for several film festivals.

Butterfly Summer

She resides at the Jersey shore with her family. *Butterfly Summer* is Toni's first novel for adults. You can follow her on <u>Facebook</u>.

ALSO FROM ELLYSIAN PRESS

The Devil's Triangle
by Toni De Palma

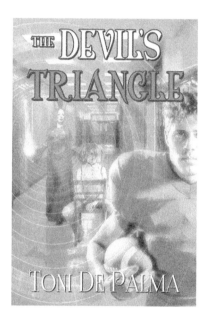

Seventeen-year-old Cooper dies in an attempt to burn down his school and awakens in the afterlife. Lucy, the Devil's sister who has crossed party lines, decides to give Cooper another shot at heaven. The deal? Cooper must return to Earth and find a girl named Grace. The rest is up to him.

While Cooper figures out his mission, he's thrown into the life he's always wanted. Great parents, a spot on the

Butterfly Summer

Varsity football team and a real future are all within reach. But what he really wants is Grace, a feisty girl with an abusive boyfriend who can pound Cooper into pulp if he isn't careful. Lucy plays demonic-puppeteer, but clues to an unknown past between Cooper and Grace start to unravel. Cooper discovers that what's keeping him and Grace apart is far more sinister than anything this bad boy could have ever imagined.

TONI DE PALMA

Aethereal,

The Alchemy Conspiracy, Book 1

by Kerry Reed

Magic versus science. Wyst versus Etruria.
The solution: a royal wedding to join the two warring
lands.

The Lady Emrys Bruma arrives at court, but not for the ceremony. Her task is to find the secret behind an old family disgrace.

She becomes entangled with the crown prince, his future bride and his best friend. Soon it is difficult to determine where her loyalties lie.

Butterfly Summer

And who can be trusted.

With spies, assassination attempts and the age-old superstition against magic, Emrys walks a fine line between two worlds.

But nothing is as it seems.

Especially the Lady Emrys Bruma.

Marked Beauty
by S.A. Larsen

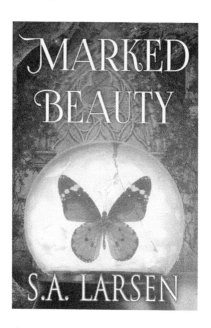

Uncovering hidden secrets can sometimes kill you . . . or worse, steal your soul.

Anastasia Tate has a secret. She can feel the emotions of others through their life energy auras. Not a welcome gift for a teenager. Especially when a sinister presence begins stalking her.

Viktor Castle also has a secret. He's tasked with protecting humanity yet cursed by an ancient evil to destroy it.

After Viktor saves Ana's life, her abilities grow stronger. Drawn together, she senses Viktor has answers to lifelong questions. Only he shuns her at every turn, knowing he has saved her only to put her in more danger.

As Ana struggles with her attraction to Viktor, he tries everything to bury his unexpected feelings for her. But they must find a middle ground. For only together can they combat the dark forces threatening both their lives . . . and their souls.

About Ellysian Press

Ellysian Press has been bringing high-quality, award-winning books in the Speculative Fiction genres since 2014.

To find other Ellysian Press books,
please visit our **website**:

You can find our complete list of **novels here**. They include:

<u>**Forthcoming**</u>

Life Indigo, Book 2 of The Water Nymph Gospels by Keith R. Fentonmiller

Evil's Dawning, Book 2, The Evil Saga by Jordan Elizabeth

<u>**In Stores Now**</u>

Company of the Damned by R.A. McCandless

Dead Alley: A Motley Education Book by S.A. Larsen

Hell Becomes Her by R.A. McCandless

Tears of Heaven by R.A. McCandless

The Desecrated by John Gray

Butterfly Summer

Yonder & Far: The Lost Lock by Matthew C. Lucas

Fate Accompli by Keith R. Fentonmiller

Evil's Whisper by Jordan Elizabeth

Beneath a Fearful Moon by R.A. McCandless

Time to Die by Jordan Elizabeth

Aethereal by Kerry Reed

The Soft Fall by Marissa Byfield

Motley Education by S.A. Larsen

Moonflowers by David A. Gray

The Clockwork Detective by R.A. McCandless

Time to Live by Jordan Elizabeth

The Moonlight Herders by Stefani Chaney

Before Dawn by Elizabeth Arroyo

Redemption by Mike Schlossberg

Kālong by Carol Holland March

Marked Beauty by S.A. Larsen

Dreamscape by Kerry Reed

The Rending by Carol Holland March

A Deal in the Darkness by Allan B. Anderson

Made in the USA
Middletown, DE
06 July 2025

10091678R00159